Paid in Karma

Meesha

Lock Down Publications and Ca$h
Presents
Paid in Karma
A Novel by *Meesha*

Lock Down Publications
P.O. Box 870494
Mesquite, Tx 75187

Visit our website @
www.lockdownpublications.com

Copyright 2019 by Meesha
Paid in Karma

First Edition February 2020
Printed in the United States of America

This is a work of fiction. Names, characters, places, and incidents either are products of the author's imagination or are used fictitiously. Any similarity to actual events or locales or persons, living or dead, is entirely coincidental.

Lock Down Publications
Like our page on Facebook: Lock Down Publications @
www.facebook.com/lockdownpublications.ldp
Cover design and layout by: **Dynasty Cover Me**
Book interior design by: **Shawn Walker**
Edited by: **Jill Duska**

Stay Connected with Us!

Text **LOCKDOWN** to 22828 to stay up-to-date with new releases, sneak peaks, contests and more…

Thank you.

Submission Guideline.

Submit the first three chapters of your completed manuscript to ldpsubmissions@gmail.com, subject line: Your book's title. The manuscript must be in a .doc file and sent as an attachment. Document should be in Times New Roman, double spaced and in size 12 font. Also, provide your synopsis and full contact infor-mation. If sending multiple submissions, they must each be in a separate email.

Have a story but no way to send it electronically? You can still submit to LDP/Ca$h Presents. Send in the first three chapters, written or typed, of your completed manuscript to:

LDP: Submissions Dept
Po Box 870494
Mesquite, Tx 75187

DO NOT send original manuscript. Must be a duplicate.

Provide your synopsis and a cover letter containing your full contact information.

Thanks for considering LDP and Ca$h Presents.

Acknowledgements

Whew, twelve books! Who would've thought I would get into this writing shit and actually accomplish something? I sure didn't. This journey has been one to remember for a lifetime. But it wouldn't have been possible without all of my readers and supporters.

Thanks y'all for riding with me for the past two years. There are many more books to come and you won't be disappointed. *Paid in Karma* is worth the read and it's wild. I hope you enjoy it, and don't forget to leave a review.

Thanks for the support!

Love ya,

Meesha

LDP4LIFE

Meesha

Chapter 1
Justice

As I rolled over in the king-sized bed I shared with my husband of one year, the chill of the sheets let me know Weston wasn't in bed with me. I glanced at the clock and it read three in the morning. Sitting up in the bed, I reached over and turned the lamp on so I could locate my phone. Before making the attempt to call my beloved husband, I looked around to see if he had the decency to leave a note explaining why he left our home in the wee hours of the morning.

There wasn't any sign of a note and it only made my temperature rise through the roof. As I held my phone in my hand, I pressed the button to go to the messages and there wasn't one from my husband. I opened Weston's contact information, hit the icon, and listened while the phone rang nonstop until the voicemail picked up.

I wasn't one to call my husband's phone repeatedly and wouldn't start at that moment. At the sound of the beep, I took a deep breath before leaving a candid message. "I don't know what was so important that you left our home without telling me, but it was very selfish of you not to answer when I called. In case you have forgotten, I am pregnant, and anything could've been wrong with me. Don't worry, nothing's wrong. Call me back before you dare step foot in my home."

Ending the call, I got out of bed and put my feet deep into my slippers. Weston had been coming home later than usual the past couple months and he blamed it all on work. This was the first time he'd ever left at this time of the morning. Wes, as everyone called him, was usually very upfront when he left the house for whatever reason.

I went into the kitchen to warm a cup of milk so I could go back to sleep. Being eight months pregnant was taking its toll on me. I pulled a small pot from the cabinet, opened the refrigerator, and grabbed the milk. After adding a little bit to the pot, I turned the fire down low and took a seat at the table. My mind drifted to the day I met Weston King.

It was a busy day at First National Bank. Everyone had decided to conduct some type of business on their lunch break that day. I was filling in at the front counter because one of the tellers had called off sick. Being a manager didn't mean I couldn't still get my hands dirty.

"Welcome to First National, how are you today?" I asked the woman as she stepped to my window.

"I don't have time for pleasantries," she shot back nastily. "I need to withdraw fifty thousand dollars from my primary account."

"Okay, ma'am. Insert your card and enter your pin, we can have that done in no time."

She inserted her card and her chip wouldn't work. After inserting it three times, her frustrations grew at a rapid pace. "This shit doesn't work! I have to get back to work, I don't have time for this!" she yelled loudly.

"May I have your card, please? I'll conduct the transaction from my end," I said, keeping my cool. The hood side of my brain was trying to activate, but I knew I had to remain professional. She chucked her card across the counter and I had to take a deep breath as I picked it up.

"Okay, Mrs. O'Neil, I have your account information in front of me and it seems like your account doesn't have the amount you are requesting available for withdrawal."

"He beat me to the bank! If your black ass would've been faster, this wouldn't have happened!" Mrs. O'Neil screamed.

At that moment, the lobby became extremely silent. Everything stopped and a pin could have been heard if someone dropped one.

"Excuse me? There's no need for any name calling, ma'am. I'm sorry there was a slight delay, but I did everything I could in a timely matter."

"Just shut up! This is all your fault!"

"Hold on a minute—" I said before I knew it.

"I'll take care of this matter, Justice." Her privileged ass was about to get handled if my boss hadn't stepped in when he did. "What seems to be the problem, Mrs. O'Neil?" he asked, glancing at the computer screen.

"This bitch—"

"Ma'am, you will not disrespect any of my employees. Now, address me about the situation and I will try my best to help you."

"Well, your employee was taking her time getting my information into the system and because of her lack of professionalism, I wasn't able to get the money I came here to retrieve!"

"Mrs. O'Neil, my manager did everything she was supposed to do. I saw the whole encounter from start to finish," Matt said, looking at the screen once more. "According to your account, you are the secondary holder on the account in question. How much are you trying to withdraw today?"

"I was trying to withdraw fifty thousand dollars, but because of her lack of training, it's no longer available," she snapped.

"That was not the case at all, ma'am. Even if the card reader was working properly, the funds still wouldn't have been available to you. Edwin O'Neil made a note on the account stating he wanted you to be removed from the account. That request is still pending at this moment, but the available balance is three dollars and fifty cents."

"He shouldn't have been able to do that! There was well over one hundred thousand dollars in that account and I want it!" she demanded.

"Mrs. O'Neil, that's something you will have to discuss with Mr. O'Neil. There isn't anything else I can help you with at this time," Matt stated calmly.

"Yes, there is. You can explain how he was able to withdraw all of my money without my knowledge."

"The way the account is set up, he was the primary account holder. You, on the other hand, were added later on. Therefore, he had every right to do whatever he chose to do with the account."

"Two signatures would've been needed to withdraw that amount of money, sir!"

"If it was a joint account, yes, your signature would've been needed. But since he's the primary holder on the account, not so much."

"Just give me all of the remaining monies out of all the accounts. I want to close them immediately!"

"Unfortunately, Mrs. O'Neil, I won't be able to complete the transaction for you. Mr. O'Neil would have to come into the branch personally to close his accounts."

"You will be hearing from my lawyer, son of bitch! I have rights! And you!" she screamed, pointing in my direction. "I should kick your black ass, bitch!"

"Leave now, Mrs. O'Neil, or I will call the police. You are no longer allowed in this establishment. I'm personally going to file a report on you and get a no trespassing order against you. Charles, escort Mrs. O'Neil out, please."

Charles, the security guard, walked over and motioned for her to leave. Mrs. O'Neil turned her nose up at him and huffed out of the door.

"Justice, I'm sorry about that. I'll call Mr. O'Neil personally to inform him about what transpired. I'll take over the front counter. Take the rest of the day off," Matt said, waving the next client over.

"Matt, I can't afford to take the rest of the day off," I whispered.

"I'll pay you for the day, Justice," Matt said before calling the next client over. "Hi, how can I help you?"

That was my cue to get out of there while I had the chance. I went to the back and grabbed my belongings from my locker. As I walked through the lobby, the many people standing in the long lines made me want to go put my things down and continue working. Instead, I shook my head and walked right out the door.

Hitting the button on my key fob, I opened the back door of my 2019 Jeep Cherokee as a deep baritone invaded my ears. "Hello, beautiful."

I slowly turned around to see who the voice belonged to and my eyes connected with a handsome god. The dark suit he wore hugged his broad shoulders to perfection and the pink shirt he wore underneath bounced off his dark complexion. My eyes surveyed his physique from head to toe and back up to the bulge in his pants.

"I wanted to thank you personally for handling the situation back there with grace. You didn't let her insults bring the worst out of you, and I like that. I'm sorry, I'm Weston, by the way," he said with an outstretched hand. Weston had me standing in front of him looking like a Special Ed student without the drool. He snapped his finger in front of my face and I flinched a tad bit.

"Sorry, um, hello," I responded clumsily, placing my small hand into his. "I'm fine. No, you're fine. Fuck! I'm Justice." With every fumbled word, my cheeks grew hotter from

the embarrassment I was displaying every time I opened my mouth.

Weston smirked and caressed my hand. The motion actually soothed me, and I felt a little more comfortable. "Thanks for the compliments you didn't mean to say out loud. You are beautiful as well. I would like to see you again. Here's my card," he said, reaching into the inside of his suit jacket and handing me the business card.

"I have to get back to work, but hopefully, I'll hear from you soon, Miss Justice." He winked at me before he turned and strolled down the street in the opposite direction.

Standing in the same spot a few minutes more, I finally opened the door and got in my truck. "Damn, that man was fine!" I yelled loudly.

Glancing down at the card, I read what was displayed on the front. Weston King, Architectural Technician at Citywide Architects. His business number was at the bottom, but I wasn't going to call him right away, even though I wanted to call and leave a message for him to listen to when he arrived back at his desk. Thinking it over, I decided to tuck the card in the side of my purse and headed home.

I did end up calling Weston three days later. We went out to dinner, and our chemistry was magnetic. He proposed after three months of dating, we were married two weeks after that, and I found out I was pregnant three months after we eloped.

The bubbling of my milk brought me out of my daydream and I hopped up to turn the fire off. I poured the hot liquid in a mug and sat down to let it cool for a bit before I attempted to drink it. The life Wes and I shared together had been going great until a couple months ago. He worked at a prestigious architectural company and he was usually home between five and six in the evening.

On the night in question, he was home on time, but I wasn't feeling well and had gone to bed early. Now I was awake in the middle of the night and my husband was nowhere to be found. I picked my mug up by the handle and waddled back to my bedroom to see if Wes had called or texted me back. There were no missed calls or anything on my device and my anger turned to worry. Calling his mom was something I refused to do because I hated involving other people in my business.

Slowly sipping the warm milk, I called around to hospitals all over the city and the city morgue. There was no one by the name of Weston King brought in to either place. After an hour, I stopped trying to track down my husband and the anger was back. Deep down in my soul, I had a feeling he was out doing something he had no business doing.

Crawling back in the bed, I pulled the covers over my body to get some rest before my alarm went off alerting me to get up for work.

Meesha

Chapter 2
Wes

"Fuck, Shanell! This pussy feels so damn good!" I growled as I gripped her hips and slammed my dick deeper into her sugary walls. My toes were digging deep into the plush carpet and my balls were tingling because my seeds were swimming fast to the finish line.

Shanell squeezed her wall muscles around my shaft tightly and I couldn't hold back any longer.

"Oh yeah, shit!" I howled as I shot my load into the condom I was wearing.

Backing up on shaking legs, I tapped on her ass a couple times before I walked toward the bathroom. As I turned the water on in the shower, I glanced up at the clock and saw that it was damn near five in the morning. I hopped in the shower and quickly washed the evidence of sex off my body while thinking about the shit Justice was going to put me through when I got home.

She was sleeping peacefully when I received the explicit text from Shanell at one-thirty in the morning. Justice wasn't feeling well and had gone to bed early while I stayed downstairs watching *SportsCenter*. My phone pinged and I opened the message and the view of Shanell's pink center rocked my mans up instantly. I went upstairs to check on Justice and she was sound asleep, so I took that opportunity to sneak out.

My plan was to come over and break Shanell off and leave, but the quickie turned into a full-blown sex session. I kept telling myself to end things with her, but I didn't know what it was about her snatch, I couldn't seem to get enough of it. Even though Shanell was in the picture years before I even met Justice, I knew we could never have a life together as a couple.

As I turned the water off, Shanell entered the bathroom and pulled the shower door open. She licked her lips, and I knew she was ready for another round.

"Nell, I gotta go. We did what you wanted to do. Now I have to get home before Justice wakes up," I said before she could get anything else started.

"You gotta go? Wes, why do we have to go through this every time you come here? I still can't believe you married that bitch and still fucking me in the process! What purpose does that serve?" Shanell had every right to be upset, but she kept allowing me to come and go as I pleased. Who am I to cut off a willing participant?

"Don't start with that shit, Nell. You knew when you sent that message I was going to be in and out. You will see me again soon. Now, go take a shower. I'll lock up when I leave," I said, walking out of the bathroom and wrapping a towel around my waist.

"Fuck you, Wes! When you leave this time, don't come back!"

I laughed at her as I ran my hand down my face. "That's not gon' happen. I pay the bills in this muthafucka. Or did you forget that tad bit of information? If anybody is leaving and not coming back, it would be you. It won't happen though, and you know why," I said over my shoulder.

"Maybe I should let your *wife* in on our little secret. See how cocky your ass would be then!"

The towel I was drying off with hit the carpeted floor and I stalked back into the bathroom. Startling Shanell as she stepped into the shower, I wrapped my hand around her neck and dangled her in the air. "If you ever contact my wife, I'll beat yo' ass until you're black and blue. Don't fuckin' play with me, Shanell," I said, letting her go. Her body fell to the floor with a thud as I looked down at her angrily.

18

"Keep yo' muthafuckin' threats to yourself! You must've forgot who the fuck I was before I started wearing a suit, bitch. That nigga still rests inside me, and you're the only muthafucka that seems to push the right buttons to bring him out. Stop gambling with yo' life, because I'll cash that shit out! Like I said, I'll talk to you later." I stalked back into the bedroom and snatched my clothes from the chair by the window, hurriedly putting them on.

Shanell waltzed into the room, rubbing her throat. She stood watching me dress with a mug on her face. "This what we doing now, Wes? You feel you have to put your hands on me because of the shit you hiding from your precious wife?"

"Stop talking stupid and you won't have to worry about me putting my hands on you. It's that simple," I said, continuing to dress.

"Nigga, do what you have to do, because I won't stay quiet too much longer. I was in the picture before that bitch!" she hollered. "It was me that was carrying your drugs in my pussy, moving state to state, for you to go marry another muthafucka to reap the benefits! Me, Shanell Jones, was the one calling lawyers and putting money on your books when you were locked up, and this is the thanks I get! Karma is a bitch, Wes! You don't want to fuck with me. Keep that shit in mind."

Shanell slammed the bathroom door, leaving me standing in the middle of her bedroom looking stupid. Everything she said was true, but I didn't feel bad about any of it because she did what the fuck she was supposed to do as my woman at the time. The reason it didn't go any further was because she took it upon herself to sleep with the next nigga while I was on lock and thought I wasn't going to find out about it.

After tying my J's, I went to the bathroom door and turned the knob. It was locked and I could hear the water beating down in the shower. Not wanting to argue further, I grabbed my jacket and left. Shanell wasn't going to open her mouth about us. She loved me too much and didn't have a job to keep up with the way I had her living. She wasn't stupid by a long shot.

Driving home, there wasn't a soul on the road with me. Since it was after five in the morning, the Chicago traffic was nonexistent. I took that time to groove to the tunes of Musiq Soulchild as I cruised on the expressway. Moving Justice out to the suburbs was the first thing I did when we got married. One reason was to get away from the bullshit I used to do before I met her, and the second was to put space between her and Shanell.

Even though Shanell knew about my wife, Justice knew nothing about her. Shanell also didn't know Justice was eight months pregnant. That was something I didn't know how to tell her. Yeah, it was fucked up, but I knew she would be hurt when she found out. Like she said, she had been down for me from the beginning, and I felt I owed her for the things she did back in the day.

I loved her, but we were like oil and water. We couldn't be together for a long period of time. Our sex life was what held us together, amongst other things. Shanell would always have a piece of me as long as I lived. She didn't want for anything. I made sure her account was hit every month and even when she called and asked, I gave. The thing I was trying to figure out was why she was tripping all of a sudden. She knew I didn't want to be on any type of exclusive shit with her.

Pulling into the driveway of our four-bedroom home, I cut the engine and turned off the lights. The house was dark and knowing Justice, she was sitting in wait for me to get home. The past couple months had a nigga feeling guilty. It was the reason I tried to spend as much time as I could with Shanell without neglecting my wife in the process.

Using the excuse of working late was wearing thin with Justice. She had been asking more questions every time I said I would come home late. I grabbed my phone and checked my messages, but there wasn't one from my wife. There was a missed call and a voicemail though. I pressed the message and put the phone on speaker to listen to what she had to say.

Justice's voice filled the inside of the car and she was too calm for my liking. *"Wes, I don't know what was so important that you left our home without telling me, but it was very selfish of you not to answer when I called. In case you have forgotten, I am pregnant, and anything could have been wrong with me. Don't worry, nothing is wrong. Call me back before you dare step foot in my home."*

I was outside our home, and calling her before I stepped foot in the house was out of the question. There were times I questioned myself as to why I cheated on Justice. She was everything I'd ever wanted in a woman. She cooked, cleaned, catered to me in any and every way possible. There wasn't anything I had to ask her to do; she was always on it. She worked just as hard at her job as I did, but still made a way to come home and have dinner ready when I walked through the door.

It couldn't get any better than that, but here I was going against the grain, I thought to myself as I opened the door and got out of my midnight-black Lexus ES 300H. My stride was slow as hell because I already knew my love was hurting in the comfort of our home. As I turned the key in the lock, the alarm beeped and I hurried to punch in the code.

The house was quiet as I made my way up the staircase. With every step I took, I thought about the tears that flowed from Justice's face when she noticed I wasn't home. The door to our bedroom was closed, so I reached out and opened it slowly. Her back was facing away from the door, but I could see her breathing evenly from where I stood.

Without thought, I made my way to the bed and moved the comforter away from her body, revealing her round stomach. Kissing it softly, I spoke softly to my seed while Justice continued to sleep. "Daddy loves you. I can't wait until you are here for me to hug and kiss every day."

"Where have you been, Wes?" Justice's voice cut into my conversation with my unborn.

Raising my eyes upward, I was met with her piercing cold sleepy ones and I knew shit was about to get real. "There was an emergency at the off—"

"Save that shit for whomever you were out entertaining, okay? The smell of Zest soap beat you into the room, Wes. Since when did you ever have to leave in the middle of the night for work? Never. Whatever you are doing out in the streets, I'd advise you to put a stop to it before you become a divorcee," she said heatedly as she propped her head in her hand.

"We've been good until a couple months ago. I've kept my mouth closed because I didn't want to assume anything, but the stunt you pulled this morning told me what I already know. It's on you to decide if what's outside our door is more important than the family we are creating together. I'm going back to sleep because I have a job that I have to be at in a couple hours."

Justice turned away from me and went back to sleep. She was nothing like Shanell. Confrontation was something she didn't indulge in. But I didn't think she was going to tolerate my bullshit. I had to leave Shanell alone for a minute and love on my wife more.

After undressing, I eased in the bed beside my wife and pulled her body towards me. Justice pushed my arm away and scooted back to her side of the bed. Exhaling lightly, I laid back on the pillow and stared at the ceiling. I had to make this right, because I'd fucked up big time.

***

I was able to get two hours of sleep before I woke up to get ready for work. Justice wasn't in bed with me, so I knew she had already left out for the day. My phone started ringing as I sat up, and I snatched it from the night stand. Shanell was calling and I didn't want to talk to her. It wasn't her fault I betrayed my wife, but she was the cause. Telling her we had to chill out for a minute wasn't going to sit well with her, and I didn't have the energy to go back and forth about it.

Instead of answering, I went to the closet and chose a grey Armani suit along with a sea green shirt and a black and sea green tie to match. I didn't have to worry about ironing because my wife made sure to take care of all of those things on Sunday. All I had to do was grab and go when it was time for me to head to the office.

I went into the bathroom to wash my face and brush my teeth when I heard my phone ringing again. Continuing to take care of my hygiene, I listened as my phone rang back to back for a full five minutes. Then the text messages followed. My notifications were going off a mile a minute and all I could do was shake my head as I splashed water on my face.

Grabbing a towel off the towel rack, I wiped my face and looked at my reflection in the mirror. Justice was standing in the doorway. The way she stared at me let me know she was pissed. I thought she was gone, but I guess I was wrong.

"What are you still doing here?" I asked.

"I live here, remember? The question you need to be worried about is, who the fuck is blowing up your phone?"

"Justice, I'm in the bathroom. How would I know who's calling if my phone is in the other room?" I hoped like hell she didn't go for my phone, because there was no telling what Shanell said in those messages. "Look, I'm sorry about this morning. I love you, babe. I'm going to be straight up with you. An old friend called because she needed to talk about—"

"She? Do you really think I'm stupid enough to believe you went to a bitch's house in the middle of the night to talk?" I turned to face her, but couldn't find any words to say in return.

"You got me fucked up, Wes. I may be cool, calm, and collected, but I'm far from stupid. If all she wanted to do was talk, why couldn't the shit wait until daybreak?" She paused for a second.

"The only thing open at that time of the morning is legs. You have one chance to tell me the honest to God truth and we can get past this. If you continue to lie and I find out the truth later, it's not going to be good for you. I'm going to let you shoot your shot and it better be a good one," she said, leaning against the door jam.

"Baby, there's so much I need to tell you. Can we continue this conversation when I get home tonight? I'll tell you everything, I promise. Once we talk, you won't have to worry about anything else."

"Whatever, Wes. You better hope I'm still here when you get home," she said, walking out of the room.

I got dressed quickly and grabbed my briefcase, phone, and keys as I rushed out of the bedroom. Stepping off the last stair, I could hear Sam Smith's *"I'm Not the Only One"* blasting through the house. It further let me know this incident would not blow over any time soon. When I walked into the kitchen, Justice had her back turned and she was stirring something on the stove.

"I'll see you when I get off. I love you," I said, leaning in for a kiss. She left my ass standing there puckered up and it had me feeling like shit. Backing out of her space, nodding my head, I left the kitchen and headed out of the house.

As soon as I backed out of the driveway, my phone started ringing again. Thinking it was Shanell, I snatched it out of the cup holder without checking the screen. "What? Why are you blowing up my fuckin' phone?" I blared, pressing the brake.

"Good morning to you too, brother." My sister Bria laughed. "I told you not to marry that bitch and to stick with Shanell. Now you're going through it."

"I've told you about disrespecting my wife, Bria. Justice has never did shit to you, but you don't like her behind yo' friend," I said, backing out onto the street.

"Fuck yo' wife, nigga! Shanell was there through thick and thin and you shitted on her. For the past year, I have kept my mouth closed because you are my brother. How long do you expect me to sit back being silent? Hell nawl, I don't like your precious wife. She's stuck up and acts like the world revolves around her. Shid, you act like you forgot where the fuck you came from at times since you started working a legit gig."

"What do you want, Bria?" I didn't have time for her ghetto madness, just like I didn't have time to deal with Shanell's bullshit.

"You don't think I know you put your hands on Shanell today, nigga! That shit was foul. You are the one hiding shit from your bitch, not her. Get your shit together, because putting your hands on her on top of ignoring her calls has set her off."

"If Shanell shows up at my home, Bria, I'm fuckin' you up. I don't give a fuck how close y'all are, you are *my* sister. She is not to know where I rest my head, understood?" I said in a stern voice.

"I'm not gonna tell her where you live. But I can't stop her from coming to your job. Call her back and hear her out, Wes."

"I was gon' call her anyway. Bria, stay out of my business and slow your roll when it comes to what me and Shanell have going on. I've been telling you the same shit for years, and you still haven't grasped the concept. Mind ya fuckin' business! Now get off my phone before I forget we're related."

I ended the call and immediately dialed Shanell's number. The phone rang several times before she decided to answer. "So, you finally got away long enough to call me back? Did you read—"

"Shut the fuck up! You know better than to call my phone like that, Shanell. Why are you trying to fuck up what I have going on?"

"What you got going on? Are you serious right now? I've been allowing you to do you for damn near a year. You were crooning 'I love you' to me while trying to get to know the bitch you call your wife! She can't mean too much to you if you're always in my bed caressing my kitty. I'm supposed to just sit back and enjoy being your mistress, Wes?"

"Shanell, you've sat back this long, now it's a problem. We have to chill because my household has been affected. I have to make sure my wife is stress-free right now because this is too much for her. I'll call you; don't call me," I said, taking the phone from my ear.

"Wes, you better not hang up this muthafuckin' phone! I'll tell her everything! And I do mean everything!" She screamed loud enough to pause my thumb over the red button of my phone.

Pressing the speaker button, I cleared my voice. "Your threats don't mean shit to me. If me yokin' yo' ass up earlier didn't show you I'm not playing around with yo' ass, punching you in your shit just might. Stay the fuck away from my wife, and she better not find out shit unless I tell her. Find a fuckin' job, because you gon' need it fuckin' with me."

I let my thumb fall on the red button to end the call, I was pissed because I let her stupid ass get under my skin. My phone rang again, and it was my boss calling. "Yeah, Stewart," I said when I answered.

"Where are you? We have the meeting with Winston & Daniels Inc. in thirty minutes. Please tell me you didn't forget."

"I didn't forget. I'm on my way now and I'll be there in the next fifteen minutes."

"Okay, I'll see you soon."

Pulling up to Citywide Architects, I parked in my designated spot in the garage and hopped out with my briefcase in hand. When I got to the elevator, I pressed the button and it opened right up. Hitting the button for the fourteenth floor, I rested my head against the wall and closed my eyes. It felt like everything I'd worked so hard for was crumbling down right in front of my eyes.

When I stepped into the office, Charlotte the receptionist greeted me as I passed her desk. "Good morning, Mr. King. Your coffee is on your desk along with a blueberry muffin."

"Thank you, Charlotte. Good morning to you too." I smiled and made my way to my office.

I placed my briefcase on the desk and took a long sip of my hazelnut coffee before taking a seat. Removing the folder of the drawings I needed from the case, I sat in my chair to look them over. The drawings were miraculous to me, and the building was going to be a beautiful addition to the downtown area. While making minor alterations, there was a knock on my office door.

"It's open," I called out without looking up.

"King, my man!" my boss Stewart said cheerfully as he entered my office. "Elliot from Winston & Daniel Inc. is on his way. Are you ready to present your ideas?"

"I stay ready. You know this, Stew." Peeking at the building illustrations I had put my heart into, I smiled proudly.

"Let me take a peek," Stewart tried it. He knew no one saw my work until it was time to reveal them. Like any other business, folks loved to steal ideas of the great ones, but they would never have the ability sauce it up like the original.

"Nah, you'll see during the meeting." I smirked. "You already know how I operate, chief."

"I had to try my hand at it. Figured maybe you would give in. Anyway, are you confident with the outcome?"

"Who do you think you're talking to, Stew? I'm confident in everything I do."

The beeping from the intercom interrupted our conversation. "Yes, Charlotte. What's up?" I asked after pressing the button.

"Mr. Elliot is here for the meeting."

"Okay, thanks. Show them to the conference room and we'll be right there." Ending the call, I looked at Stewart and stood to my feet. "It's show time, boss."

"Show me what you got, man. I'm anxious to see what you came up with," he said, leading the way out of the office.

Two hours later, the meeting was over and it was successful. Elliot decided to go with my designs and was very impressed that I had the Agenda plans ready to present as well.

We went through contacting the construction company, ordering material, and financing information. With everything that took place, we were ready to work within the next four to five months. After escorting Elliot and his team to the elevators, Stewart followed me back to my office.

"King, that was a pretty amazing job you did in there. I wasn't expecting you to be totally ready to face Elliot in the manner in which you did. Winston & Daniel is one of the hardest clients to win over, and you nailed that shit. We've been trying to snag them for years, and you made it look easy. Great job!"

"Thank you. I knew I had to showcase my talent because this is not where I want to be stuck at in this company. There are bigger opportunities out there for a man like myself."

"You have totally done that, Weston. Williamson must've had faith in you, because he wanted me to give this to you after the meeting," he explained, handing an envelope to me.

I hesitantly opened the envelope and pulled out a piece of paper with the Citywide logo at the top and started reading. My heart started beating fast and my lips curled up into a smile on their own. Two years of busting my ass had finally paid off.

"Come on, King. What does it say?" Stewart asked.

"Williamson has offered me a position for Chartership with the CIAT. I was waiting for the opportunity to manage projects on my own from start to finish. I've finally proven I could do just that!" I exclaimed, pumping my fist in the air.

"You deserve it, man. Congratulations, and welcome to my world. We have to celebrate your accomplishments soon. For now, wrap up the loose ends to get started on the next step of this project so you can go home and enjoy that beautiful wife of yours. I have work to do myself, so I'll see you later."

After Stewart left, I sat behind my desk and called Justice. When she didn't answer, my excitement went down a notch. While I was trying to share my great news, she was still upset about the dumb shit I had pulled that morning. My desk phone rang and the smile returned when I saw who was calling.

"Citywide Architects, this is Weston King speaking, how may I help you?" I greeted the caller in my business voice.

"Get the fuck outta here, nigga! Put my big brother Wes on the line." My brother Donovan laughed. "Yo' ass needed me to make you laugh, I see. The caller ID let you know it was me."

"You're right. I knew it was you, brah. How's things in Cali?"

Donovan cleared his throat before responding. "Cali is Cali. There's so much going on that I had to get away. The li'l niggas on the west coast is ruthless. I'd rather deal with the shit in Chicago before I get caught slippin' away from home. That's the reason I called. I've decided to move back home, Wes."

Donovan, known on any street as Dap, was my younger brother. He was conceived while my parents were married, and it started a riff in our household. Regardless, we were raised together as if we had the same mother. Donovan decided to move to California four years prior and he stacked his paper legally and illegally.

My little brother was a big-time drug dealer that got his money hand over fist by selling the purest dope around. He also started his own business called Customs by Dap. The business started in our father's basement with custom T-shirts. He had since ventured out to jewelry and he was a hit around the world.

"That's what's up. When are you packin' up to make the move? I can take some vacation time off and help."

"No need. I'm already in the Chi. I really wanted to surprise you, but thought against it. I've been getting everything in order for the past couple months. Now I'm good. I handed the empire down to Juice because I've molded him into a mini me for that purpose. I'm done with the street life. I'm making more money legally anyway."

"How the hell are you gon' run Customs by Dap from Chicago? And how long has your ass been here?" The disappointment of not knowing my brother's moves while they were in the making was evident in my voice.

"Yesterday. I had to close on a house that I've had my eye on and decided to come on through to sign the paperwork. I'll be staying at my mom's crib until I can furnish my shit. As for Customs, I hired an entire team to run the joint for me. They've been doing an excellent job thus far."

"Mm-hmm," I said, listening.

"I'll still be hands on because majority of the shit can operate online. My big money clients know to contact me by phone, and I'll fly wherever to get the cheddar. Plus, I've been thinking about expanding here. Finding a location has been a problem though."

"Damn, bro, you on yo' shit. I'm proud of you. If I can help in any way, I'm here. It's good to have you back." The line was silent for a spell and I thought the connection was lost. "You still there?"

"Yeah, my bad. I was responding to a text. How is the married life?" he asked, getting back to the conversation.

"Dawg, shit was sweet until I fucked up."

"What the hell you do? Ain't shorty about ready to deliver my niece or nephew?"

"Not quite. Justice is eight months, man. I went out to see Shanell—"

"You still fuckin' with Shanell's trifling ass?" he asked, surprised. "I thought that shit was over and done with years ago. Do she got crack in her pussy, whereas her shit keeps calling you, nigga?"

"I'm done with her. She threatened to tell Justice about us and I choked the fuck out of her ass. Now I have to go home and tell my wife everything before she hears the shit from someone other than me. The thing is, I haven't told Justice about my past and I don't know how."

"Wes, you keeping secrets from your wife? That's not a good look, brah."

"I know."

"In any relationship there has to be trust or you have nothing. Especially in a marriage. Be straight up with her, because you don't want to lose your family behind Shanell. She ain't worth it. I know she was there from the start, but she did you dirty when you needed her the most."

"Dap, I know what she did, okay? Sometimes I feel bad about what happened to our child while I was away. I owe her for that."

"You don't owe her a damn thing! She's holding that shit over your head to keep you in her life. She fucked a whole nigga that was supposed to be like a brother to you while carrying yo' seed. Fuck that bitch! It wasn't your fault she lost the baby, bro. Stop letting her manipulate you."

"I hear what you're saying. It's— I don't even know. Shanell and I are finished. We already established that when she called earlier. There's nothing to worry about."

"Hopefully you're right. Look, I have to go. We'll catch up soon. I have to meet my sister-in-law. It seems I came home at the right time. Tell her everything, bro. She gon' be hurt, so be ready to pack yo' shit until she's ready to forgive you. Leave no stone unturned," Dap said, ending the call.

It took fifteen minutes for me to get my mind back on work. I even tried calling Justice again, but the results were the same as before. Losing my wife wasn't an option. I had to fix this shit, and fast.

Meesha

Chapter 3
Tana

"Tomorrow we will have a test on chapters five and six in your history book. Also, the essay on 'What are your future goals and ambitions?' is due upon entry first thing in the morning. Continue to be great. I am proud of each and every one of you. Class dismissed."

Being a teacher at Culver's Elementary was a challenge in itself, especially with eighth graders. I was glad the day was over because I was exhausted from the previous night's shenanigans. Tyson, my boyfriend of three years, decided our relationship wasn't something he wanted to continue. Any other female would've been crying and fussing. Not me. I didn't even dwell on the why. I have never been in the profession of keeping a man that didn't want to be kept.

"Ms. Taylor, how was your day?"

Snapping out of my thoughts, I turned my head toward the doorway of my classroom. Mr. Davidson found his way to my class at the same time every day, trying to convince me to go out with him.

"My day was fine, thanks for asking. What can I help you with, Sir?" I asked, even though I knew what he wanted.

"What's your plans on this lovely Thursday? I was thinking if you didn't have any, we could go out for an early dinner."

"Mr. Davidson, I've told you time again I'm in a relationship. Besides, I never get involved with anyone I work with on a daily basis. Sometimes business and pleasure doesn't mix." Gathering my things, I started stuffing everything into my briefcase.

"We can't even go out as friends, Montana?" The way he pushed the issue was irritating my soul, but I tried my best to contain myself and keep it professional.

"We are colleagues, Mr. Davidson. Nothing more. I don't use the word friend loosely. It's a title that's earned. Working together doesn't automatically constitute us being friends. There's a hidden agenda on your end and I'm here to tell you, we will never cross that line. Have a good day."

Lifting my jacket from the back of my chair, I walked past him. Once he realized I had nothing more to say, Mr. Davidson stepped aside and allowed me to lock up. "Enjoy the rest of your day, beautiful," he called out as I made my way to the main office. I threw my hand up and kept trucking down the hall.

Upon entering the office, I noticed one of my students sitting in a chair with her hair all over her head. "Keturah, what happened?" I asked, taking a seat beside her.

"Brandy said she wanted to fight after school, so I gave her what she wanted. Now she knows I'm not the one," she said with no remorse in her words.

"Keturah, we've talked about this before. You cannot continue to let your anger get the best of you. It's not hard to walk away from negativity. I know it's easier said than done because I was fourteen once too. Your main focus needs to be graduating. The grades are there, but your conduct will look really bad on your records. High school is worse than this, sweetheart."

"I understand what you're saying, Ms. Taylor, but when there's somebody constantly talking shit and then has the balls to run up, what was I supposed to do, run the other way? Nah, that ain't happening. Brandy tried to stunt for her crew and I stomped her ears together."

"Language, Keturah. When conflict shows its face, go tell someone. Stop it before it escalates into something more."

"Then I'd be labeled a snitch! The niggas that killed my brother didn't snitch and got away with the shit! Fuck these people, nobody cares anyway."

"Watch your mouth. I'm not going to tell you again. That's what's wrong with society now. Nobody wants to tell the things that's going on. Instead, everyone wants to handle situations on their own." Hearing the words Keturah spoke was sad because she wasn't the only kid with the same mindset.

"I'm sorry about what happened to your brother, Keturah, but you have to do what's right in order to better yourself. You're always talking about getting out of the hood. You can do it. You will do it! It's all about believing in yourself and leaving the bull crap where it's at." I tried my best to make her understand the logic in what I was saying.

"Telling a teacher about negativity isn't called snitching. It's protecting yourself. When you're ready to change your mindset, come see me. Until then, try to stay out of trouble."

Keturah had rolled her eyes and turned her back to me in the middle of me talking to her, but I continued anyway.

I stood up and signed out for the day, leaving Keturah sitting in the office. She had so much potential, but she allowed her anger to get the best of her. After losing her older brother to gun violence, she developed an "I don't give a fuck" attitude. I wasn't going to give up on her, but at the same time, I wasn't going to try harder to make her see things from a positive perspective.

When I stepped outside and hit the button to unlock the doors to my car, Tyson was leaning against it with a bouquet of flowers in his hand. I felt my face harden instantly. "This negro got his nerve coming to my job with his bullshit," I mumbled to myself. Approaching him, I saw he had the biggest smile on his face, and it confused the hell out of me.

"Hey, I got these for you," he said, holding the flowers out towards me.

I walked around the car and placed my briefcase in the backseat. "Tyson, why are you here? The adamancy of breaking up was strong on your end last night." I stalked back to where he was and stood directly in front of him because I needed to look him in the eye.

"Look, baby—"

"I'm no longer your baby. You diminished that title when you said we were done."

"I really wasn't thinking when I said that shit last night, Tana. We've been together three years and I love you. The reason behind it all is this, I've met another woman. To be real about the situation, she just wasn't you. I've spent a year hoping—"

"A year, Tyson! You've been in a whole other relationship while with me? Explain where the love comes in for me. Don't worry about it; there's no need. It's obvious there is no love on your part. I'm your fuckin' comfort zone." I laughed.

"Being second best to anyone is not something I would knowingly subject myself to. The love I have for me is too strong to settle. You made your choice when you opened your mouth and said it was over between us. Then to find out you were entertaining another. Yeah, I'm going to let you stand on your decision."

I got into the driver's seat, pressed the start button, and brought the engine to life. Tyson tapped on the window, so I lowered it a little bit.

"Tana, I love—"

"Get your ass away from my car before I run yo' ass over!" I snarled as I threw the gear in reverse. "Stay your grimy ass away from me. I will not give you the chance to keep playing with my feelings like Stevie Wonder plays the piano. Go make the shit work with whatever bitch you were trying to mold into a replica of me. The success rate is going to be zero, but give it your best shot." I peeled out of the parking lot and left his stupid ass standing there with a handful of flowers.

The entire twenty-minute drive to my apartment, Tyson blew up my phone. Ignoring each call, I pulled into my complex parking lot and threw the car in park. Snatching my phone from my purse, I checked all the messages he left and deleted all of them. There was no way I was going to allow him to disrupt my life.

I unlocked the door, threw my briefcase on the sofa, and started taking my clothes off as I made my way to my bedroom. Frustration was at an all-time high because Tyson actually thought I was a simple-minded bitch. It proved he didn't know anything about me after three years of being together.

After tossing my clothes into the hamper, I went into the bathroom to shower. I stepped inside the tub, and the way the water beat against my body was relaxing. After washing the day's mess away, I dried off and threw a pair of leggings and a crop top on. I made my way to the kitchen and removed the ground beef from the refrigerator to make tacos.

As I placed the meat in the skillet, my phone rang from the bedroom. After quickly adding the rest of the beef, I raced to grab my phone. By the time I got to it, I missed the call. Heading back to the kitchen, I pressed the button to see who was calling when I received a text from my bestie Justice.

Justice: Are you busy?

Instead of texting back, I decided to return her call. Listening to the phone ring, I got up and got my iPod Pro earbuds out of my bag.

"Hello?" Justice said when she answered.

"Hold on a minute," I said, loud enough for her to hear. Placing the earbuds in my ear, I grabbed my charger and went back into the kitchen and plugged in the charger. "Okay. Sorry, I'm trying to cook and I need both hands, so I had to get my earbuds. What's happening, bestie?"

"I just needed to hear your voice." Justice was quiet for a bit and she wasn't her usual bubbly self.

"Jus, what's the matter? Talk to me, sis," I said, picking up the spoon moving the meat around the skillet.

"I think Wes is cheating on me."

"Come again? That man is not cheating on you, sis. From what I see, he worships the ground you walk on."

"I haven't said anything about this, but the past couple months, Wes has been moving differently. He would usually get home around six-thirty, give or take, and if he had to work overtime, there would be no hesitations when he told me." Clearing her throat, she sighed before going on.

"Lately, he has been coming in later than usual without letting me know beforehand. Then last night I wasn't feeling good so I went to bed early and left him downstairs watching TV. When I woke up in the middle of the night, he was no-where to be found. He had the nerve to walk his ass in after five this morning."

"I know you lying! Where was he?" I asked, stirring the meat in the skillet.

"When I asked, he told me he would tell me everything when he got home tonight. I didn't get married to go through this shit, Tana."

"Oh wow. The only thing I can say is hear him out. Maybe he's going through something and really didn't know how to talk about it. That doesn't necessarily mean he's cheating, Justice."

"He said an old friend called because she was going through something. I don't have a problem with him helping anyone out, but why couldn't it wait at least until a decent hour? Maybe we got married too fast. I don't know."

"Again, don't jump to conclusions. Listen to his explanation and go from there. Another thing, there's no time frame on when one should marry. Love is love and y'all chose to get married after dating a short time. So what? Time waits for no one, sis."

"You're right. I just don't see any good coming from this though. I have a feeling our lives won't be the same after today," she sniffled.

"Stop crying. Stress is something you don't need right now. There's a baby inside of you that should have you smiling through any and everything. Do you want me to come over?"

"No. I'll call you back, he just came in. Keep your phone on though," she said, hanging up.

Justice and Wes was cool together and I couldn't believe they were going through trials and tribulations so early in their marriage. Hell, they were still newlyweds with a baby on the way. I hoped it was just a misunderstanding and things got back to the way they were because I believed Wes was good for my best friend.

Meesha

Chapter 4
Justice

I sat up in bed and waited for my husband to make his way upstairs. My baby took the opportunity to start kicking and moving. Rubbing my stomach, I had to lean to the side a little because the shit hurt. Wes walked into the room as I grimaced in pain.

"Are you alright over there?" he asked, walking into the room taking his suit jacket off. Laying it across the foot of the bed, he took a seat next to me and started rubbing the other side of my belly.

"Yeah, your child is just being extra. How was your day?" I asked.

"It was a good day, actually. I aced my presentation and we got the contract with Winston & Daniel. I also got a promotion. But that's not what I want to talk about. We need to discuss what happened this morning," he said unenthusiastically. I nodded my head, and he continued.

"Justice, there's so much I need to tell you about my past life. It's only right that you hear everything from me rather than someone else. Back in the day, I was deeply involved in the streets. The woman I was dealing with at the time was my best friend as well as the love of my life. She was there for me through thick and thin until I got locked up," Wes said, staring deeply in my eyes.

"I was sentenced to four years in prison for a gun charge and an attempt to distribute narcotics. Shanell was six months pregnant when I went away. Anyway, word got back to me that Shanell was fuckin' with one of my best friends. When I confronted her about it, she denied the shit. It wasn't until she lost our child the next month that she came clean about what she did." I sat quietly fighting the urge to interrupt him.

"I spent the rest of my time in prison alone. The guilt of not being there when she lost the baby ate away at me. When I got out, I went back to college and obtained my architecture degree. My record was expunged and I was ready to live a righteous life. Shanell was going through so much that I was compelled to help her."

I listened to him tell his story and was shocked because I never knew about him being in jail. I had done a thorough background check and if he hadn't told me about it, I would've never known. This Shanell person was dead wrong for sleeping with his friend while pregnant with his baby. I don't care if he was locked up, that's something you just don't do as a woman.

"So, you helped her, how?" I asked.

"I helped her get a place of her own because she was living with my sister and I also opened her a bank account. Started her off with ten thousand, I also give her money every month to make sure she'd be alright."

"Let me get this straight, you are still giving this woman money even though she lost the baby that y'all conceived together? What sense does that make, Wes?"

"I feel obligated to help her, Justice. She doesn't have a job."

"That's your fault too, huh? The magical answer I want to hear is, are you still fuckin' her?"

Wes dragged his hand down his face and his shoulders slumped slightly, but I saw that shit.

"I was still sleeping with her, but I cut her off completely earlier today."

"Wes, why would you marry me when you still had feelings for someone else? What did you think you were going to gain from that bullshit? If you weren't ready to settle down, all you had to do was talk to me. The truth outweighs a lie any day," I said, leaning forward as far as my belly would allow.

"That's not it at all, Justice. I fucked up, okay? I'm sorry." Wes grasped my hand and I gently pulled away.

"Fucked up is right. I didn't get married to call it quits. Marriage shouldn't be thrown away, even if it looks like garbage. I have to come first in your life as well as you first in mine. This union should be our focus; nothing else. We have a baby on the way and you're out there holding on to something that lives within you every minute of the day." I found myself getting upset and calmed myself down.

"Your dedication was to your baby, not to its mother. That should've been a done deal the day you decided to ask me to marry you. Since you didn't do it on your own, we will do this shit as husband and wife," I said, tilting my head to the side.

"What are you talking about?" he asked nervously.

"*We* are going to let your little friend know that her money train just came to a halt. The only way you would continue to pay her monthly would be if there was a child involved. There isn't one, and you will no longer give her money out of our household. I don't care about the place she lives, because I already know you are paying for her to live there as well. She doesn't have a job. That stops today!"

I was pissed, but I didn't want to go all out with it because there was a way to do certain things. If I showed my emotions, I'd end up busting his shit wide the fuck open and I wasn't on that. Yeah, he cheated, but I bet he was going to think twice before he tried it again.

"Justice, you don't know Shanell. I already told her we were done when she called this morning. You are pregnant, and if I take you around her, she's going to try to fight you."

"Do I look like I give a fuck about her getting mad? I'm pregnant, not crippled. That bitch bleeds just like me. Just like you were in the streets, so was I. That's the reason I won't judge you on your past, because I know how shit goes out there," I said, swinging my legs out the bed.

"The only difference between us is, I've never got caught doing the shit I did back in the day. So you can be worried about her ass, but I'm not," I said, getting up and going to the closet. I pulled a grey jogging suit from the hanger, slipped the pants on, and threw the sweatshirt over my head over the T-shirt I was wearing.

"Justice what are you doing?"

"Wes, this shit is not about to go on any longer than it's been going on. You thought I was kidding when I said it ends today? We are about to settle this shit once and for all." I walked back into the closet and took my nine-millimeter from the lock box and tucked it under my protruding stomach. Then I slipped my feet into my white Nike sneakers.

"Baby, we don't have to do this," he said softly in my ear as he wrapped his arms around me from behind.

"What is it that you're not telling me, Wes? There's a reason you don't wanted to tell this bitch it's over in my presence." His heart was beating a mile a minute against my back. That was a clear indication he was a nervous wreck. "Don't tell me she doesn't know about me."

"It's not that. She knows about you—she just doesn't know you're pregnant."

I laughed as I shook my head. "Is that so? Well, she's about to find out tonight. Let's go," I said, walking out of the bedroom with only my phone in hand.

***

It seemed like we were driving forever trying to get to his friend's house. We got close to downtown Chicago and I turned and gave his ass a side-eye stare. I knew damn well he didn't have this bitch housed in one of these high-priced-ass high rise apartments. We pulled up to an underground garage and he pushed a button on a remote he got out of the armrest and I almost knocked his fuckin' head off.

"You got to be kidding right now, Wes."

"Justice, don't put your hands on me again. I pay the bills here so I'm entitled to have access."

"Not after today, nigga. All this shit is going to be returned to the owner. If she can't afford this muthafucka, she has to get the fuck out. You ain't paying another dime."

"I understood when you said it back at the house. Would you please calm down before we go up here, man?" he asked as he pulled into a parking spot.

Without responding to him, I got out of the car and walked to the elevator and pushed the button. He finally got out of the car just as the doors opened and I stepped on. West punch the button for the fifteenth floor and the inside of the car was quiet as hell. When the doors opened, he stepped out and grabbed my hand before leading the way down the hall. Stopping in front of the door that read 1508, he stood there looking goofy as fuck.

"Use your key to open the door or knock," I said angrily.

When he didn't move fast enough, I did the honors for him and rapped on the door three hard times. I heard shuffling on the other side of the door, then silence. A door closing could be heard and I glanced over at my husband to see his reaction, but the turn of the locks got my attention.

"You must be out of your mind, Wes. What are you doing here?" the woman I'm going to assume was Shanell asked, looking me up and down. She paused at my protruding stomach. "She's pregnant!" she shrieked.

"Shanell, that's not what I came here for. Out of respect for my wife, I'm not paying your living expenses anymore. The only reason I've paid for the past five years is because the loss of our child weighed heavy on your mental state. It's time for you to move on, because I have."

Shanell chuckled without taking her eyes off me. "Clearly I heard the bullshit you said when I called this morning. Wes, you went home and did damage control by telling your wife what you wanted her to hear. Did you fill her in on how you were gripping my hips while giving me deep strokes?" she smirked. "Or did you explain that we've been in each other's lives for the past nine years and I'm not going anywhere?

"Shanell, that shit is unnecessary," Wes said, trying to cut her off, but she was on a roll.

"Wait, here's another one, wifey! Your husband and I have been sleeping together the entire time y'all have been together until this morning. Tomorrow, you can officially claim him as your husband because he's been our man for the past year."

Shanell's rant didn't produce a reaction from me and the look on her face showed she was pissed. I didn't have time to go back and forth with her and it was something she obviously wasn't used to. She wouldn't understand because it was something only real women could relate to.

Back in the day, I would've punched her in the mouth, but she wasn't solely to blame. My husband had his hand in the bullshit as well. Even though I hadn't known the longevity of their sexual encounters, I still didn't give her what she was hoping for.

"None of what you disclosed was a shock to me. The importance of coming here was to be sure you knew. This is it. The other shit you spoke of is irrelevant. You and I are not the same, sis. If this man decided to leave me tomorrow, I wouldn't look for him to make sure I was straight. I'm a go getta. You're a dependent," I said calmly.

"Bitch, ain't shit over! Wes knows what it is between us and nothing will change. He's only saying this shit because you probably gave him an ultimatum. Watch me have the last laugh. My bills are gonna still get paid by your husband and your dumb ass will continue to cry when he comes home late from work."

"I've never shed a tear when it came to Wes. But you are going to cry a river when you realize for the past five years you should've been trying to better yourself instead of sitting back allowing a man to pave the way for you."

Shanell lunged at me and Wes grabbed her before she could attack. He in turn received the blow intended for me, but it didn't faze him at all. "Are you out of your fuckin' mind, Nell? That's my pregnant wife you're trying to assault. That shit is not about to go on. You need to slow your roll before I have to lay hands on you!"

"Wes, you know how the fuck I am. You should've thought about that before you brought your side bitch to my crib! Maybe if I slap the fuck outta her, she'd stay out of my business. I don't give a fuck about her being pregnant. Her muthafuckin' face ain't carrying that baby, nigga," she said, swinging over his shoulder.

"She's far from the side bitch, and that's why you're mad. It's over, Nell. All this other shit is uncalled for," Wes said, continuing to push her back. "Have a seat, man! You won't get any closer to her."

"Let me go, Wes!" Shanell screamed.

A door in the back of the apartment opened and a tall, caramel complexioned guy emerged with a white wife beater and basketball shorts on. "Shanell, what the fuck—" He paused when he noticed Wes holding her by the arms.

"I told you not to come out here! You just put more fuel on the fuckin' fire, Curt!" Shanell had tears in her eyes for the first time since Wes and I showed up at her home. "Wes, it's not what you think," she calmly said as she turned to face him.

Wes looked between the two of them with hatred in his eyes. I didn't know who the dude was, but Wes wasn't too happy to see him. His eyes went back to Shanell. She had her head hanging low and she was quieter than a church mouse.

"You mean to tell me you got this nigga laying up in the crib I've been paying for? What type of shit is this, Shanell?" Wes's voice boomed through the apartment.

"He just came over to check on me!" she cried.

"You don't have to lie to this nigga!" Curt said, pointing at Wes. "What the fuck you crying for? He got married and left you out here to fend for yo' muthafuckin' self! If it wasn't for me, you wouldn't have shit." Wes pushed past Shanell and stalked toward Curt. She jumped between them to stop whatever was about to happen.

"I don't know what she told you, but I didn't leave her without shit! I've been providing for her ass on the strength of our child, homie. The last thing you want to do is come at me about some shit you know nothing about. Yo' bitch ass violated when you were fuckin' her behind my back!" Wes barked.

"Continue to support her ass, because she gon' need it. I want yo' shit out of here come Monday. Let *this* nigga find you a place to lay your muthafuckin' head. The stress of worrying about your mental state is something I no longer feel obligated to do. You can slit your muthafuckin' wrist if that's what you choose to do. Don't call me for shit!"

50

When Wes turned his back, Curt pushed past Shanell and I pulled my nine quickly. "You may want to think about that before you're carried out of this bitch in a body bag," I sneered. Wes stared at me before moving forward to take the gun from me.

"Let's go," he said, grabbing me by the arm.

But I shrugged him off as I walked backwards away from the door. Wes led me toward the elevator, but I kept my eye on what was going on behind him.

"I see you done went out and married a gangsta bitch. Teach her the fundamentals about pulling a gun without using it!" Curt yelled out.

"Wes, I'm sorry!" Shanell cried from behind us.

"Shanell, if you don't clean yo' muthafuckin' face!" I heard Curt snap before the door slammed.

Wes was damn near dragging me down the hall towards the elevator. I felt Curt and Shanell were going to be a problem for my husband. But Wes had to prove our marriage was what he wanted, because I wasn't about to be fighting and bickering over someone that made vows to love me 'til death.

Meesha

Chapter 5
Wes

Justice was silent the entire ride to the house. I knew she was pissed, and she had every right to be. When Curt showed his face, my first thought was to fuck his ass up. Shanell was playing me for a fool, and she would've kept it going if we hadn't popped up at the apartment. I'd been feeling sorry for her monkey ass the whole time and this nigga been right there with her.

It had nothing to do with him still smashing her. The two of them probably spent countless hours laughing at me while spending my money. Shanell got two thousand dollars out of me every month. Not anymore though. Since she had Curt's ass finessing her, I was going to contact the management office first thing in the morning. The lease was up at the end of the month anyway.

All the crying she did back there was a front. Maybe the tears were real, but I really didn't give a fuck. There were many things I could do with the funds she would no longer receive from me. The most important issue at the time was my marriage.

Glancing over at Justice, I had to break the ice to see what her thought process was. "Bae, say something. We have to talk about this."

"Wes, you had a year to talk about this shit and you chose not to! What do you want me to say? For you to be a street nigga, you played yourself back there." Justice grilled the side of my face and I could feel the heat resonating off her.

"All the shit your *lil friend* said didn't upset you, because where was the lie? The anger didn't surface when I was called every bitch in the book, nor did it really show up when she lunged at me. But the minute that nigga emerged from the bedroom, it was another story. Explain that shit, because I'm not understanding at all."

Justice shifted in the seat as much as the seatbelt allowed propping her fist under her chin. I was trying to play everything back in my mind to see things her way, but I was drawing a blank. For her to say I didn't get mad was crazy, because I was ready to beat Shanell's ass when she took a swing at her.

"Justice, that's far from the truth. I did everything I was supposed to do to protect you and my seed. Yes, I was furious when Curt came out, and it was justifiable. That nigga was foul back in the day and he's foul now. When I was on the street, this nigga ate when I ate and he violated when he slept with my woman!"

"And he's still fuckin' the bitch while making you look stupid today! You don't ever turn your back on a nigga that stabbed you in the back before. Shanell got you forgetting everything you learned surviving in the streets. They are going to be a problem, Wes!" I shouted.

"I didn't sign up for this bullshit! We have been married one year and you fucked up! I won't sit here and place blame on the woman you decided to cheat with. That was a decision you made. Your loyalty was supposed to be with me, and it seems she got just as much of your affection as I did"!

"I'm sorry, Justice. I promise, I'm going to make this right. Nothing like this will ever happen again."

"It shouldn't have happened in the first place! What the fuck were you thinking?"

The tears that ran down her face tugged at my heart. Seeing my wife cry was something I vowed to never put her through and here I was doing just that. "Baby, stop crying. Things weren't supposed to go the way it did with Shanell. Obviously, I wasn't thinking. It was a mistake."

"A mistake? An entire year is a mistake? Shanell is a woman that you spent years of your life loving, Wes! How can you open your mouth to say it was a mistake? The two of you shared so much with one another and now I'm here competing with the love of your life!"

Justice was mad and I saw the veins protruding from her neck when I glanced at her. "Your vows said that I was the love of your life and I've seen it's far from the truth. Fix the mess that you've made, Wes. I have a headache. Just get me home, please," she sniffed.

"We are going to talk about this, Justice. I'm not going to let you shut me out, dammit!"

"Keep the same energy you've had for the past year. If you had been straight up with me from the beginning, we wouldn't be where we are today. Being sneaky about shit like this don't automatically grant you a get out of jail free card. It doesn't affect only you, Wes. I've been subjected to this bullshit involuntarily! You need to give me time to myself."

"Justice, you are pregnant. You can have all the time you want within the comforts of our home. Don't think about leaving."

"Did you fuck that bitch in the comfort of our home? No, you didn't! Leave me alone while you can, Wes. This is not the time for you to throw your head of household status around. I'm going to do whatever I feel fit and there's nothing you can do nor say about it. You're lucky I haven't said I'm done with your muthafuckin' ass!"

As I pulled slowly into the driveway, Justice already had her hand on the door handle. Before I could put the car in park, she was out of the car and wobbling up the steps to the front door. Knowing I fucked up royally, I didn't even try to stop her. My mother's words echoed in my ears as I sat in the car.

"Wes, Shanell needs help. There's nothing you can do on your own to get her through this. Don't mess up your life trying to save hers."

Now look at me. I'd jeopardized my marriage on many levels for someone that really didn't give a fuck about me. My mother was going to curse me from here to Jerusalem when she found out what I'd done. As far as she knew, I had stopped messing around with Shanell when I met Justice. Which was far from the truth.

After entering the house, I locked the door behind me and went searching for my wife. Justice's voice could be heard bouncing off the walls as I climbed the steps to our bedroom. "Tana, I can't believe this is happening to me!" she cried. "If I would've known I had to fight to keep my husband, we could've just been common law partners for the rest of our lives."

"You love him, right?" Her best friend Tana's voice bellowed out of the speaker.

"My love is not in question. You should be asking Wes if he loves me!"

I walked into the room and my wife was pacing back and forth throwing clothes into a duffle bag. "Justice, if I didn't love you, I wouldn't have married you. Shanell was a mistake."

"Tana, come get me. I expect you to be here in less than a half hour," Justice said, ending the call.

"Leaving is not going to solve our problems, babe. We need to talk about this."

"There's nothing to talk about right now, Wes," she said, rubbing her stomach. The gesture made me quite nervous because I knew Justice was stressed and it wasn't good for the baby. "You left our home on many occasions to keep your past in our present. If nobody understands where my mindset is right now, you should. I'm not giving up on our marriage. I just need time to think things over."

It hurt my heart to watch my wife pack clothes to leave our home. The fault of it all was all on me. I wanted to debate more about her staying, but that would lead to more stress that she didn't need. My phone vibrated in my pocket as I stared at Justice's back. I pulled it from my pocket and it was my brother.

"What's up, bro?" I asked as soon as I answered.

"Come let me in, I'm at the door."

"I thought you had business that needed to be handled."

"I did, but there was this feeling I couldn't shake telling me to come by and make sure you were good."

Dap always had a premonition when it came to me and ninety percent of the time, he was right. Taking another look at my wife, I turned to head downstairs to let my brother in. Pulling the door open, Dap stood looking just like our father.

"Damn, man. If I didn't know you were out here, I would've thought you were Dad coming to my crib," I said, embracing him in a brotherly hug.

"Let me find out you been missing a nigga," he said, stepping back a little bit. "You look like you lost your best friend. Oh shit, did I interrupt your talk with Justice?"

"Nah, come in. We just came in a few minutes before you called," I said, walking to the bar.

"Y'all went out for dinner, so I assume everything went well. Pour me a shot of Henny."

"Dap, we didn't go to dinner. Justice wanted to go to Shanell's to hear me break things off in person. You know how Shanell is and she tried to fight and shit, but you knew I wasn't letting that happen. Shanell was talking all her shit until that nigga Curt came out the back. Then she wanted to cry all of a sudden."

"Hold up! That dirty muthafucka still in the picture? I told you she was using yo' ass, brah. I bet Curt was helping her just like you were. Are you sure that baby was yours?" Dap asked, taking a seat on one of the bar stools.

"Dap, don't go there, bro, because you will make me go back over there and kill that hoe. Justice pulled her pistol on Curt because he tried to run up on me when my back was turned."

"Why the fuck would you turn your back on his ass? He's not to be trusted at all like that. You been out the game too long but the rules still apply. I'm disappointed in you, Wes," Dap said, shaking his head. "It's embarrassing that your wife had to save yo' ass in front of that muthafucka."

Justice took that moment to come down the stairs. Dap stood from his seat and smiled. "Hello, Justice. Nice to finally meet you," he said, looking at the bag she had draped over her shoulder. "You're leaving?"

"Who are you?" she asked softly.

"I'm Donovan. Wes' brother. I've heard so much about you."

"I've heard a lot about you as well. It's good that you're here to keep your brother company. Maybe you can give him some advice while you're in town. He really needs it," she said, shooting an evil glance in my direction.

"Wes understands what he has done was wrong. He really loves you, Justice. Don't let this mess with Shanell break up your home. She doesn't mean anything to my brother. Shanell has held the loss of their baby over his head for years," Dap said sincerely.

"One thing you will learn about me is, I speak nothing but truth. My brother was a fool for Shanell and should've ended that shit long ago. Believe me when I tell you, I was pissed when he told me he got out of prison and still helped her after all she did to him."

"I'm not giving up on my husband. Leaving for a little while is the best thing for me to do because if I stay, Wes will get his ass beat every time I think about the shit he caused. I'll be back once I clear my head of this bullshit."

"You don't need to leave this house to do that!" I snapped.

"Lower your tone when you're talking to me, Wes. I'm not the one that you should be raising your voice at. Chastise yourself before you come for me. None of this is my fault, so don't blame me for putting myself first for a change!" Justice roared pointing in my direction.

"I've done nothing but love you and in return, you disrespected me behind my back and loved me in private. This is not the fight you want. I promise."

Before I could respond to what Justice said, the doorbell rang. She headed for the door and snatched it open. Tana tried to walk inside, but was pushed back out and the door slammed behind my wife. Jumping to my feet, I yanked the door opened and stepped on the front porch, but the only thing I saw was the back of Tana's car going down the street.

"Give her time to clear her mind, Wes. This situation is a lot to handle and she has the right to feel the way she does. There's no need for me to keep saying 'I told you so'. Shanell got yo' ass once again. Come on so we can go get a drink and something to eat," Dap said from behind me.

Meesha

Chapter 6
Shanell

"So, you were still fuckin' with that nigga after you said y'all was done, Shanell?" Curt asked after he snatched me back into the apartment.

The tears I was shedding in the presence of Wes dried up when he ignored me as he led his bitch down the hall. "That's none of your business! You don't have a right to ask me anything! You are in a whole relationship and all we do is fuck. Know your role in my life and play that shit accordingly."

"What the fuck you mean I don't have a right to question you? I've been doing more than just fuckin' you, Shanell! You're actin' like one of them reality show hoes right now."

I laughed because both of them niggas were lacing my pockets and didn't even know it, putting their relationships in jeopardy for the sweet shit between my legs. Neither one of them wanted to be with me and I was cool with that as long as I got paid.

"Just what I said, Curt. You did what you wanted to do for me. I didn't ask you for a damn thing. Everything is good over here. If you would've stayed your ass in the room, Wes wouldn't have even known you were here. But no, you had to throw it in his face that you were still involved with me. You can leave now," I said, going into the kitchen.

The relationship I had with Wes was all good until he ran off and eloped with his now wife. He forgot all the shit I'd done to hold his ass down then popped up on the scene with a damn wedding ring on his finger. My feelings for him hadn't wavered until I became second in his life. That was the reason I started testing how far he would go to still be a part of mine.

The text I sent him was done purposely because I knew he would find a way to my apartment. I did everything I could to make sure he lost track of time, and it paid off. What I didn't see coming was his wife standing by his side.

"Shanell, playing with me is the last thing you want to do," Curt sneered as he came into the kitchen behind me. I continued rustling around in the refrigerator to find something quick to eat as I ignored what he was saying.

Curt grabbed me by the back of my neck and brought my head out of the box and roughly forced me to face him. "Bitch, I will break yo' fuckin' neck! You are playing a dangerous game! That shit will get you and that nigga killed. You told me y'all haven't spoken since he got out and here it is you lied! Now tell me why you felt the need to do that!"

"Get your hands off me, Curt. I'm not your little girlfriend, so I advise you to get your shit and get out of my house." As I tried to pry his hand from my neck, his grip became tighter, but there wasn't an ounce of fear in my heart.

"I'm not going anywhere until you tell me what I want to know!"

"Okay! When I tell you, leave my shit and don't come back. I've been fuckin' Wes since he came home and he pays all the bills here. You happy now? Your money was an added bonus because I don't want for anything because Wes makes sure of that," I said snidely.

"From the looks of things, after tonight, you're on your own. I hope you saved for a rainy day," he said angrily, shoving me into the cabinet before leaving the kitchen.

"Aaaagh!" I belted out holding my side. There was a knife on the counter and I didn't think twice about gripping it in my hand. "Don't you ever put your hands on me, muthafucka," I yelled as I jabbed him in the right side of his torso.

"You crazy, Shanell!" he said looking down at the knife sticking out of his body. "I can't believe you stabbed me! And for something yo' stupid ass did." Curt rushed to the bathroom and wrapped a towel around the knife before entering my bedroom and retrieving his keys and cellphone.

"Come here, let me take the knife out and clean you up."

"You're out of your mind. I'm not bleeding to death behind you! Lose my number with your looney ass." Curt pushed me to the floor and ran out of my apartment while I laughed the entire time, hoping he passed out and died on the way to his car.

I went back into the bathroom and got the bleach from under the sink. Curt left blood drops all over the carpet and I had to get it up before it stained. It took me about an hour to clean up his mess and in the process, I prayed he didn't come back, because I didn't have a problem finishing the job. My mind flashed back to the day my stepfather put his hands on me for the last time.

It was a hot summer day and I had come home after curfew. My mother worked nights and I knew my stepfather would be asleep. Creeping into the house, I kicked off my shoes so I would be able to sneak in my room without him hearing me. As I made my way across the living room floor, the light illuminated the room.

"Where have you been, Shanell? It's after midnight and you were supposed to be home at nine," Greg asked, getting to his feet. "You are sixteen years old. Everything is closed at this time of the night."

"I was at Marsha's house. Now, can I go to bed? I have school in the morning," I said, walking past him swiftly. Greg grasped my forearm tightly and pulled me back in front of him.

"You're a liar! Marsha came by here right after school looking for you. Do you want to try again? This time I want the truth! Your mother's probably at work worried to death because you weren't here when she left."

"My daddy has been dead since I was two! I don't have to explain nothing to you," I sneered.

Greg reached back and smacked me across the face. My head whipped to the side and I could taste blood inside my mouth. Looking up at his six-foot frame, I spit the blood in his face, causing him to punch me on the top of my head. The stars that danced in front of my eyes blinded me for a few seconds and my head started pounding.

"I am your fuckin' daddy! I've spent my money on your rebellious, spoiled ass your entire life and you have the nerve to tell me where the fuck that bastard is! I know exactly where he's at. I was the one that sent him to meet his maker!" he yelled, pushing me onto the sofa.

Greg stood over me and grabbed me by the face. "Your curfew is nine o'clock! Don't ever come in my house smelling like a whore ever again! Tell that nigga I said stay the fuck away from you. I have no problem beating you until your ass is bruised all over, Shanell. Go your ass to bed, and you better not mention anything to your mama!"

My blood was boiling over and all I could see was red. Standing from the sofa, I walked slowly to the back of the house where my room was located. Greg was moving about in the living room as I stood in front of the mirror examining my face. There weren't any visible signs of him hitting me and I was glad because I didn't want to have to explain anything to my mother. The door to my mother's bedroom slammed shut about fifteen minutes later and I sat on my bed and waited.

I took my clothes off in the middle of the room and walked to the closet. Taking the wooden box from the top shelf, I removed the hunter's knife that my boyfriend had given me for protection and twirled it around in my hand. As I eased my bedroom door open, Greg's snores filled my eardrums as I walked slowly toward the room he shared with my mother.

Greg was lying on his back with his hand in his pants when I opened the door slowly. His mouth was wide open and the room smelled like corn chips. I walked around the bed and the moment Greg raised his hand to hit me replayed in my mind. Swinging my arm back, I brought the knife down on Greg's throat and pulled it back with force.

His blood splattered on my naked body, but I didn't flinch. Instead, I used my free hand and rubbed the blood into my skin. Laughing uncontrollably, I stood watching Greg's blood seep out of the open wound onto the pillowcase he was lying on. Without any remorse, I left the room and went straight to the bathroom and climbed into the shower as his blood flowed down the drain. I slept like a baby until I heard my mother scream at the top of her lungs when she found Greg's body.

I laughed to myself about what I'd done to Greg. That night would forever be embedded in my mind. I had my lie already memorized, but when the police asked me what happened, I told the truth with a little white lie. I told them Greg had raped me and hit me in my mouth. The cut inside my mouth was proof as well as the fact I had sex that night. But it didn't get me off the hook.

I spent six months in juvenile detention and two years in a psychiatric facility. Majority of my time was spent trying to convince the doctors there was nothing wrong with me. No one believed me and I was constantly fed high doses of lithium, antidepressants, alprazolam, better known as Xanax. The medication fucked me up more than me killing Greg, to be honest.

The females in the facility got a taste of whoop ass every day and I stayed locked down for the first year. Once I learned how to beat the system, I knew I was going to get out of there sooner than I was supposed to. I became the face of being re-formed and everyone was proud of me. Little did they know, I just wanted out.

A week before my eighteenth birthday, I was sent to a half-way house because my mother wanted nothing to do with me. She had a restraining order against me and I couldn't contact her at all. One month after I turned eighteen, I was given an envelope which contained twenty thousand dollars. My coun-selor explained that my mother left the money for me to get on my feet once I was healthy enough to live on my own.

Instead of looking for an apartment, I went straight to the bus station and randomly picked a city and bought a ticket. I did eeny meeny miney moe and Chicago was the lucky winner and Philadelphia was a distant memory. I hadn't seen nor heard from my mother since I was sixteen. That was eleven years ago.

I climbed into my bed, and my phone rang as I got com-fortable under the covers. Reaching over to the nightstand, I glanced at the screen to see who was calling and it was Bria. Wes must've called his sister and filled her in on what hap-pened.

"Hello," I said, lying back on my pillow.

"What's wrong with you, Nell?"

"Huh? I don't know what you mean, Bri?"

"Hoe, have you taken your medicine today? You sound more like the crazy bitch that lives within you. I know you're not letting the bullshit with Wes get to you. He'll be back. Let him cool off."

"Bria, it's over between us. Wes and his bitch came to my apartment tonight. I tried to beat her ass and he played captain save a hoe," I said, getting mad all over again. "And why the fuck you didn't tell me she was pregnant?"

"I live in Michigan, Shanell! How am I supposed to know what's going on in Chicago?"

"That's your brother! You know everything else but you didn't know he had a baby on the way? Stop lying to me!" Bria was really pissing me off because she really thought I was stupid.

"Calm down. I didn't tell you because most of the time you don't know how to act. I'll admit, Beverly told me five months ago."

"And that's when you should've been telling me! I had to find out tonight and looked like a fool in the process. Not to mention, Curt brought his ass out—"

"Curt? Please tell me he wasn't in that apartment, Shanell. When did you start fucking with him again?"

"He's been paying my bills for the past six months. It's a done deal though. The muthafucka put his hands on the wrong one. I hope he bled to death before he could get to the hospital."

Bria was silent for a spell before she spoke again. "What exactly did you do?" she asked after taking a deep breath.

"I stabbed his ass! He was choking the fuck out of me, what was I supposed to do?"

"You need to take your medicine. I know you haven't been taking them because you are out of control. Curt shouldn't be anywhere near you because you know the history with him and Wes. Not to mention, you are the reason they are at odds. Look, I have to go. Take care of yourself and call me if you need me. Stay away from my brother, Shanell. I'll talk to him and then we can figure something out."

If Bria hadn't hung up before allowing me to respond to the bullshit she said, she would've known I had no plans of

leaving her brother alone. Lying back on the pillow, I got comfortable while thinking about all the shit I was going to do in
order to fuck up Wes and his wife's lives.

Chapter 7
Tana

The shower I'd taken, plus the lasagna I ate when I got home from work had me feeling good lying in my bed. There were plenty of papers I needed to grade sprawled on the bed beside me, but I kept dozing off like a crackhead. My phone rang and jolted me awake and I was kind of glad it did. Moving the papers around until my hand connected with it, I glanced down at the screen and Justice's picture stared back at me.

"Hey, Jus," I said, rolling over.

Justice went into a rant about Wes while crying her heart out. The two of us had been more like sisters since the first grade and I could count on one hand how many times I'd heard her cry like she was. When she told me to come get her, I jumped up and threw my sneakers on without changing out of my pajamas. Grabbing my keys, I was out of the house and in my car in a matter of minutes.

I didn't know what happened, but it had a lot to do with Wes coming in at five in the morning. My speedometer was touching seventy miles an hour on the residential street because Justice wasn't anything to play with when she was mad. I spotted a police car up ahead and slowed down even though there was nothing they could do to me because they already had someone pulled over. When I hit the expressway, I punched the gas like I was in the Batmobile.

It took twenty minutes for me to get from the city to the suburbs where Justice resided. There was an unfamiliar Beemer with California plates parked in their driveway. I was curious to know who the owner was as I stepped out of my car. Hurrying up the steps, I pressed the doorbell and waited for someone to answer. Justice snatched it opened and pushed me back as I tried to enter.

"I wanted—" I started to say.

"Nah, we out," she said, slamming the door and walked quickly down the steps.

Knowing not to question her, I made it to the car and pulled off once she was inside. As I drove back to the expressway, the silence was deafening inside the car. The only sound that could be heard was Justice's phone continuously pinging from the text messages that were flooding through. She refused to even look down at the phone to read the content. Instead, she stared straight ahead through the front window.

"Whenever you're ready to talk, I'm all ears," I said, breaking the silence.

"This is one for the books. I'm twenty-six and I've never been the type of female to fight over any man," Justice said, shaking her head.

"Start from the beginning. What happened?"

"Wes has been fuckin' a woman he was with for nine years. Her name is Shanell and she lost a baby while he was serving time in prison. Mind you, I didn't know anything about him being incarcerated until today," Justice explained in a steady voice.

"He has changed his life, so his imprisonment doesn't bother me. He got out and opted to help her financially, but what he failed to do was cut the bitch off when he got involved with me. Wes left his ass out of our home to fuck and came back to me as if I was going to be cool with the shit. When he came in from work, I listened to his explanation and got dressed. He was nervous as hell when I said let's go."

"Wait, where did y'all go?" I asked, taking my eyes off the road briefly.

"Fuck you mean? We went to pay her ass a visit!" She proclaimed. "Tana, this bastard has been paying for this hoe to live downtown in the AMLI Lofts on Clark Street. Those apartments are at least two thousand a month for a fuckin' one bedroom! Mind you he's doing this for a muthafucka that cheated on him with his best friend!"

"Oh, hell nawl! I can't believe Wes is that stupid. This Shanell person would've been living in a one bedroom on the south side for six-fifty! What the hell was he thinking?" I asked seriously.

"He claims the loss of their unborn baby was messing with her mental state and he felt obligated to help her. For five years? Nah, I'm not buying that. Her unemployed ass won't be living like the Joneses any more. I believe Wes would've given her time to find a job if his former best friend hadn't waltzed in from the bedroom."

"I know you fuckin' lying! She's still sleeping with the nigga she was cheating with while Wes was on lock?" The things Justice was revealing were a shock to me. I wouldn't have believed a word of it if it hadn't come from my best friend's mouth.

"Yeah, gold digging-ass bitch. I put all the blame on Wes because he was the one that said 'I do' before God. Shanell tried to fight when she noticed I was pregnant. If Wes didn't jump in front of me, I would've tagged that hoe, big belly and all."

"This shit makes me look at Wes in a different light. He was cool with me until he pulled this bullshit. What are you going to do, Jus?"

"I'm going to have my baby and live my life. Shanell is going to be a problem and I'll be ready to stomp a mud hole in her ass when the time presents itself. This is just the beginning, and I know Shanell is going to try her best to tear our marriage apart. In the meantime, my husband needs to think about what he has done and figure out what's more important in his life."

Justice tapped her fingers repeatedly on the window while shaking her head. "I've packed enough clothes to stay with you for a while, if that's okay with you. I don't want to go to a hotel by myself. I'd rather stay with you in case I have to go to the hospital."

"Don't insult me, Jus. My door is always open for you. I do want to say this, y'all need to talk and lay everything on the table," I said.

"Tana, if you could've heard half of what I said to Wes, you would know I'm not playing with his ass. I'm riding this marriage thing out, but he will learn to cherish me as the wife he chose to be with."

I pulled into the parking lot of my complex and was lucky to park in a spot in front of the entrance. We got out of my car and I opened the back door, taking Justice's bag from the backseat. Leading the way to my apartment, I unlocked my front door and placed the bag on the table.

"Have you eaten? I have some leftover tacos in the fridge," I asked, making my way to the bathroom.

"Heat some for me! You know I'll eat tacos even if I've eaten already. What else did you cook with it?"

"Black beans and yellow rice," I said, walking out of the bathroom drying my hands. Tossing the paper towel in the garbage when I entered the kitchen, I pulled all the food out of the refrigerator to feed my best friend.

Justice was quiet so I peeked out of the kitchen to see if she was cool. She was sitting on the couch typing away on her phone. Maybe she finally read the text messages that were hitting her phone in the car. Leaving her alone, I went back to the kitchen and heated up her food.

As I waited for the microwave to sound, my phone rang and of course it was Tyson. I ignored the call and went scrolling on social media to see what type of drama was taking place. In the process, my phone started ringing again and I decided to answer to see what his goofy ass wanted.

"What, Tyson?" I asked, agitated.

"Damn, Tana! Why do you have to answer the phone like that? Would you please hear me out?" Tyson begged.

"There's no need because I'm done. There's no way for you to fix what you wronged. You wanted out and I gave it to you. Now leave me alone. Go be with whomever you thought would be a better me than me." I chuckled.

"Baby, I'm sorry. You are the love of my life and I realize I've made a huge mistake. The thought of being with Rachel was great in the beginning, but after a while, reality really sank in."

"We got a name!" I said cheerfully. "Tell me more about Rachel, Tyson," I said, acting like I gave a damn.

"Come on, Tana. I'm being truthful here and you're mocking me for this shit."

"I'm not mocking you. I want to know about your sweet Rachel," I explained as the timer on the microwave sounded. Placing the plate on a tray, I got a bottled water out of the fridge and walked to the living room with the phone cradled under my chin.

"Rachel is one of my coworkers," Tyson explained as I partially listened. "Everything was good until I met her parents and I was judged the minute I walked through the door."

"And why would they judge you when they didn't even attempt to get to know you?" I asked as I handed Justice her food. She looked up at me and mouthed "who is that?" Holding up one finger, I sat on the loveseat by the window and waited for him to respond.

"They judged me because I'm black."

"Come again? You mean to tell me you went out and cheated with a white woman and thought you would get Montana Taylor from her? Sorry, you were sadly mistaken." I laughed as I got up and turned my back to Justice.

"Now I'm mocking you, Tyson. That is the funniest shit I've ever heard in my life. You experienced racism up close and personal and you thought coming back to me was going to be successful. I got news for you, Tyson, you thought wrong. You better go back to Becky with the good hair and figure that shit out."

"I don't want her! It's you that I want, Tana."

Tyson sounded pitiful and I was no longer laughing at his dumb ass. At that point, I wanted him to know I wasn't entertaining his foolishness another day. He fucked up when he thought he would find someone better than me.

"Don't call my phone anymore. I won't change my number, block you, or any of that immature shit that women do nowadays. I'll embarrass your ass whereas you would never be able to show your face in this city again. We are done! I can't believe you thought a white woman would replace me. You are a fucking joke. Goodbye," I laughed, ending the call.

Justice sat with her mouth opened in shock when I turned around placing my phone on the coffee table. "When the hell did all of this take place?"

"Girl, with all the shit going on with you and Wes, I forgot all about Tyson's clown ass. As you heard, he has been fucking with a white chick from his job for a year and ended things with us last night. He recently met her parents and they don't like his ass because he's black. Now he's back trying to get his Keith Sweat on saying he's sorry and she's not me. Nigga better go to Walmart and buy him some toys to play with and leave me alone."

"Damn. You don't even seem bothered about it."

"Bitch, I'm not! It's his loss. I don't have time for the back and forth shit. I've never had a problem bagging a man and it won't stop at Tyson Brooks. The three years I wasted with his ass is the only problem with all of this. I'm cool."

"That's good," Justice said, stuffing her face. "He lost a good one for sure. He should've known in today's society, there's too much division to try the interracial thing."

"Girl, fuck Tyson. He'll figure that shit out sooner than later, without me. Wes bought a new Beemer from California?" I asked, changing the subject.

"No, why would you ask that?" she asked, taking a sip of water.

"There was a black Beemer in your driveway with Cali plates when I picked you up. If it doesn't belong to y'all, whose ride was it?"

"Oh, I didn't even pay attention to that shit. It had to be Donovan's car," she said, throwing the last of her taco in her mouth.

"His brother? No wonder you prevented my ass from entering. You didn't want me to see him." I playfully hit the side of her head and put my hands on my hips.

"Nah, I pushed you out because I was ready to leave that house before things got ugly between me and Wes. Donovan was the last thing on my mind." She grunted as she stood from her seat. Justice was in the kitchen washing her dishes when her phone chimed.

"Your phone is going off!" I yelled.

"It's only Wes begging and pleading like he's been doing since I left. He isn't saying anything I want to hear right now," she said, coming back in the room. "I'm about to go to bed, I'm sleepy as hell. Thanks for coming to get me. I really appreciate you."

Justice grabbed her bag from the table by the door and snatched her phone from the sofa as she headed toward the guest room. "Oh yeah, Wes is going to come by to drop my car off tonight or in the morning. If he comes before you leave for work, do not let him inside your apartment, Tana. I don't care what he says. Goodnight and I love you, bestie."

She said all of that as she made her way down the hall so, I didn't get the chance to respond before I heard the door close behind her. It was after eleven o'clock and I knew the papers I was supposed to grade wouldn't get done. Good thing I already put tomorrow's test together for my students because I was going my ass to sleep too. I'd had a very long day of pure drama and I was over it.

Chapter 8
Wes

Last night was horrible for me. Shanell really showed her ass and I wanted to fuck her up. I stayed up half the night texting and calling my wife without really getting a clear response from her. Donovan didn't make things any better because he chewed my ass out about how stupid I was for fucking with Shanell after all she had done. No one would ever understand why I stood by her side.

I met Shanell downtown when I had to go downtown to the County Clerk building to get a duplicate of my birth certificate. She was sitting on a bench with a small backpack, looking lost. Her beauty was what caught my attention, but I rushed inside the building to take care of my business. The last thing I wanted was to be in there all damn day.

It took about forty-five minutes to get the document and I rushed out looking for shorty. Noticing her sitting in the same spot, I smiled, walking toward her. The sun danced off her chocolate skin and there were beads of sweat running down the side of her face. The ponytail she had her hair in was disheveled and messy, but it didn't take away from her natural beauty.

"Hey, beautiful. I saw you sitting over here and thought I'd come over and speak," I said, standing before the mystery beauty.

"Hi." That was all I got from her and then she turned her head away from me.

"Can I sit down and get to know you? My name is Weston, but everyone calls me Wes. And you are?"

Rolling her eyes, shawty ignored me and refused to talk. I wasn't willing to give up because I wanted to get to know her.

"I'm a good dude, you know. It's hot out here, how about I treat you to lunch so we can get out of this heat?"

"What makes you think I want to go anywhere with you?"

"It was an offer. I mean, it's hot out here and I want to get to know you and put a smile on that pretty face of yours. You are too beautiful to be frowning the way you are. That causes wrinkles, you know," I said, trying to lighten the mood.

"There's nothing to smile about, to be honest."

"Well, let's talk about it while we get something to eat. I promise I won't try anything. Pick the spot and we're there."

"I don't know anything about this city. I chose Chicago randomly and didn't think about what I would do once I got here."

Hearing her say that had me more intrigued to hear her story. She was alone in my city and I knew I couldn't leave her out there by herself. "How about we start over. I'm Wes," I said, holding my hand out to her.

"Nice to meet you, Wes. I'm Shanell." She smiled and shook my hand.

From that day forth, me and Shanell were together all the time. Shanell explained what happened after she got off the bus at the rest stop. She was buying food and was mugged when she walked out of the fast food restaurant. A guy was watching her without her knowledge and saw the envelope full of money she had in her hand. Placing the money in her purse, she walked out to get back on the bus and he pushed her to the ground and took off with her purse in hand.

That led to her telling me why she was carrying so much money and how she had nowhere to go in the big City of Chicago. Me being the man I was, I got her a hotel room not too far from one of my traps for a couple months. During that time, I made sure she had everything she needed while getting to know her.

Shanell and I became an item without even trying because we were together a majority of the time. She became very special to me to the point I stopped fucking with all the women I used to toggle around with. I eventually moved her in my place and brought her into my world. Teaching her the ins and outs of the drug game was a piece of cake because she caught on fairly quick. From that moment on, we were dominating the streets together.

Things went downhill when I was sentenced to four years in prison. Shanell was the woman I gave my all to and it hurt like hell when I found out she betrayed me while I was on lock. That was when everything went from sugar to shit.

Glancing at the clock on the bedroom wall I shared with Justice, I saw that it was five in the morning. I knew there was a lot I needed to do before going to work. With my wife at her best friend's house and me alone in our bed, I didn't get much sleep at all. Staring at the ceiling, I made a conscious choice to call out of work. I picked up my phone and shot Stewart an email letting him know I wouldn't be in.

Everything that transpired between me and my wife ran through my mind as I laid in bed. Whatever I needed to do in order to get my marriage back on track, I was ready to conquer it head on. The first step was to contact the management office at the apartment building where Shanell lived. I couldn't do anything until nine o'clock, so I turned over and went back to sleep.

I was woken up by the ringing of my phone. Rolling over, I fumbled around on the nightstand until my hand connected with the device and answered without opening my eyes. "Yeah," I said groggily.

"Wes, I'm sorry for what I did. Curt only came over to see if I was alright," Shanell cried on the other end of the line and

I sat up, rubbing my eyes. "I wasn't going to tell your wife about us. You didn't have to come over to my place."

"Shanell, make this your last time calling my phone. There's nothing to discuss because the shit is over and done with. I don't give a damn what you have going on with Curt. Make it last forever. Far as my wife, let me worry about that. Everything is out in the open at this point. I hope you are packing your shit because it's go time for you, and I don't mean that in a good way."

"Are you seriously going to put me out? We have been through so much together and you're just going to throw it away?"

"Stop trying to guilt trip a nigga! That's all you've been doing since I touched down and the shit won't work anymore. I see your true colors loud and clear, Shanell. You don't give a fuck about me. The only thing you're worried about is the stability I provided in order for you to live comfortably without having to punch a clock."

"Wes, I don't think you want to carry out the plan with your wife," she said in a demonic voice.

Shanell went from pleading to wicked in a split second. When she lost our child, she was diagnosed with bipolar disorder, but I didn't believe that shit. Shanell didn't show any signs of a problem until she didn't get her way. I believed the medication was a front to make me soften the way I handled her.

"You don't want to play this game with me. I can make this easy on you, or we can get down and dirty. It's up to you, Mr. King."

"Do whatever you feel you have to do, Shanell. I'm too grown for games and I won't indulge in any of your bullshit. What we had is no more. This will be the last time I'll stress this to you. I have a wife that makes me happy and it was

80

wrong for me to continue entertaining you behind her back. Justice is who I want to spend forever with. You have to respect that, Shanell."

"I don't have to respect shit! Both of you muthafuckas will see that your deception put both of y'all in danger. You want to play hard ball, Wes? Let's play. You will regret the day you ever met me. Next time do a thorough check of the bitches you lay down with. I was the wrong one for you to cross."

Shanell hung up on me and the words she spat flooded my mind, but I wasn't going to dwell on it. She wasn't on shit and I wasn't worried about her. I dialed the number to the management office, I waited for Heather to answer.

"AMLI Lofts, this is Heather speaking. How may I help you?" she asked cheerfully.

"Good morning, Heather. This is Weston King from apartment 1508. The lease is up at the end of the month, but I want Shanell Jones to vacate the premises on Monday."

"Mr. King, you are correct, the lease is up at the end of the month, but in order for you to terminate the lease, you would have to still pay a portion of the fee." The sound of Heather typing away on the computer could be heard as I waited for her to continue. "You would have to pay a termination fee of eight hundred dollars to break the lease."

"That's fine. I'm willing to give you my card number—"

"I'm sorry to cut you off, Mr. King, but you would have to come down to the office with a check or money order to make the payment. Also, there will be a thorough walk-through conducted of the apartment and any damages done to the apartment will have to be paid immediately."

"There shouldn't be any damages, but don't hesitate to give me a call if there is. If Ms. Jones isn't out by Monday, you are to escort her out like it's an eviction. I'll be there with the check within the hour. Thank you, Heather."

"No problem, Mr. King. It was a pleasure having you guys as tenants. Sorry things didn't work out."

"It wasn't you guys at all. But I'll see you shortly," I said, ending the call.

Getting out of bed, I headed to the bathroom to handle my hygiene. As I turned the water on in the shower, I heard my phone chiming back to back. Curiosity got the best of me and I went back to my bedroom to see what the hell was going on. Opening the messages, every one of them was from Shanell.

Shanell: I'm going to make your life a living hell! Why the fuck did you tell them people I had to get out!

Shanell: Call them back and tell them you made a mistake, Wes!

Shanell: You think you're going to just have me out here homeless, nigga? What the fuck is your problem?

Shanell: I got something for yo' ass!

Shaking my head, I walked back to the bathroom and stepped under the hot water. Shanell was out of her mind thinking I would stop the process of her moving out of the apartment. When I said it was over, I meant just that. It was time for her to put on her big girl panties and make shit happen on her own from this point on. My marriage was on the line, and if I was going to lose my wife, I was eliminating her ass too.

Justice wanted nothing to do with me and I didn't blame her. The only thing I could do was give her the space she needed to think about everything as a whole. I got out of the shower after washing thoroughly and dried off my body. Spraying a little cologne on my neck and chest, I went to my closet and pulled a pair of grey sweats and a white t-shirt from the hangers. Pulling a pair of boxers and socks from the drawer, I sat on my bed and my shoulders slumped slightly.

Standing to my feet, I slipped on my underwear and my sweatpants. After dressing, I brushed my hair and put my watch and Cuban link chain and bracelet on. My phone rang and I knew in my mind it was Shanell's ass again, so I didn't bother to answer. When it rang again, I got agitated and snatched it up after stalking to the other side of the room.

"What?" I boomed into the phone.

"Damn, nigga! What's your problem?" Dap laughed in my ear.

"My bad, bro. Shanell's been getting on my nerves this morning and I want to choke a booger out her ass."

"Don't let that bitch get to you. She gon' be on the dumb shit for a minute. What time do you need me to come over to drop the car off to Justice?" he asked.

"Fuck, I forgot all about that. Come through now. I was just about to head out to the management office to pay the money to get out of the lease at Shanell's place."

"A'ight, I'm outside. We can roll in my whip and I'll chauffeur your ass around while we're out. I'm guessing you're not working today, huh?"

"Nah, I called out because I have to get this shit handled expeditiously."

"Alright, TI, I hear ya." He laughed.

"I'm on my way out so get off my phone, big head bastard."

"Yo' daddy." He laughed again, hanging up.

I grabbed my keys and made my way down the stairs. My stomach growled, but I didn't have time to eat anything. A banana was going to have to do the trick until I could grab some food. Dap was sitting bobbing his head when I exited my home and locked up. Opening the door to lean inside, the music blared from the speakers and I didn't know how the hell he sat inside with all that shit pounding in his ears.

"Yo' ass gon' go deaf having that shit so loud," I screamed.

"What? What you say?" Reaching over, I turned the knob on his radio and he slapped my hand down. "Don't touch nothing! Now, what did you say?" he asked

"I said turn that shit down, nigga! How the hell the music can't be heard outside of this car?"

"Oh, nowadays the law wants to pull a nigga over for every little thing. I had my whip soundproofed so I wouldn't have to deal with that petty ass shit. The noise doesn't bother me, but I see you sensitive as hell and don't like the way I bump the old school."

"That's not it. I want to be able to hear when I get old. You are gonna be deaf before you're forty." I laughed.

"What the fuck ever. Don't wish that shit on me, muthafucka. Where are we going first?"

"I guess you can follow me to Tana's crib so I can drop Justice's car off."

"A'ight bet," he said turning his music back up.

I opened the door to Justice's car and got in and backed out of the driveway with Dap behind me. Tana lived in the Hyde Park area so it took about twenty minutes to get there because traffic was light. Pulling into a spot close to the entrance, I got out and rang her bell. I knew Justice was there because Tana had to work and I didn't see her car. I pushed the button again and got the same result so I pulled my phone out and called my wife.

"Yes, Wes," she answered as she yawned.

"Why didn't you answer the door when I rang the bell?"

"I'm in bed and I don't feel like getting up. I told you last night to park the car and keep going. I'm not ready to see you right now. I thought we agreed on that already."

"Is it asking too much for me to want to give my wife a hug?"

"It's not too much to ask; it's just not going to happen. Have a good day at work, I'm going back to sleep."

Justice ended the call and I wanted to call back, but I didn't want to stress her out. Instead, I put the phone in my pocket and waltz over to Daps ride. As I got in, he lowered the volume on the radio. "Where to, boss?" he asked in a French accent.

"Yo' ass stupid," I laughed. Dap always knew how to lighten the mood when it was dark. "We are heading downtown so I can pay this fee. Hit Lakeshore Drive and head downtown."

"Bro, please tell me you didn't have that hoe in one of those high-priced ass apartments in the middle of downtown?"

"Dap, I used to live in the muthafucka at one time as well. I just let her stay after I moved out. If I would've known Shanell was going to be on all this bullshit, she would've been gone a long time ago. This is a fucked-up thing to say, but I'm glad she didn't have that damn baby."

"Wes, you knew what the hell Shanell was capable of. When you told me she was taking antidepressants, I've always said her ass was crazy way before she lost the baby. I'd bet all the money in my account that hoe been crazy all her life. You better be careful, because this shit is far from over. Being that you are my brother, I'm here for you every step of the way."

"Shanell ain't gon' be on nothing. She knows I'm still the same nigga from back in the day. I've just learned to suppress that shit."

"That's your problem, bro. You think you know her, but you don't. There's missing links in her story and you overlooked every aspect of her because you were blinded by pussy. You're not the same nigga. You live in a different world and are making great money, legally. Leave all the street shit to me. You don't need to get your hands dirty over her dysfunctional ass. I won't hesitate to slump her if it comes down to it."

I gave Dap turn by turn directions to get to Shanell's apartment. He parked in front and I got out. As I entered the building, I could hear shouting coming from the manager's office. Rushing in the direction of the loud foul language, I knew my presence was needed to rescue poor Heather from Shanell's ghetto ass.

"Bitch, I've been living here for the past five years! How the hell can he tell you to put me out? Weston King doesn't even live in this muthafucka!" Shanell screamed.

"I—I have to do what I'm told by the leaseholder, and that is Mr. King. Whatever is going on between the two of you has nothing to do with AMLI Lofts, Ms. Jones. Mr. King wants to terminate the lease, and I have to honor his request. You would have to address Mr. King with your concerns," Heather tried to explain.

I stood in the door way for a second before making my presence known. Heather looked like she was on the verge of tears and her knuckles were white from the grip she had on a ballpoint pen. I guess that was the weapon she was going to use if Shanell pounced on her.

"Shanell, do you always have to show your ass? You already know that Heather is only doing her job. All you had to do was contact me about any questions you may have. There's nothing you can say or do to make me change my mind about the decision I've made."

"The only reason you're doing this is because of your ugly-ass wife. What the fuck do she have that I don't?" she asked with her hand on her hip.

"She has me, and that's why your ass is upset. Instead of being down here harassing people, you should be upstairs packing your shit," I gritted, turning my attention to Heather. "When does she have to vacate the premises?"

Heather looked at Shanell and her eyes shifted back to me nervously. I turned to look at Shanell and she was mugging the woman as if she was going to kill her. "Heather, when does she have to vacate the premises?" I asked once more.

"Um, um," she said, clearing her throat. "I put in the paperwork for her to be out by Monday. If she isn't out by noon, she will be arrested for trespassing."

"Arrested? Bitch, I'll beat yo' white ass! You ain't gon' have me shit!" Shanell said, charging toward Heather.

I grabbed her by the back of her neck like a dog and shoved her away from Heather. "You gon' run up on the wrong somebody and get yo' ass whooped. Take yo' ass upstairs before I fuck you up!" All that professional shit went out the window when she started acting like she was in the Robert Taylor projects.

"Neither one of y'all need to worry about me. I'll be out of this muthafucka tomorrow! Wes, you gon' see me, and I mean that shit!" Shanell yelled, storming out the office.

"Should I call the police, Mr. King?" Heather asked.

"No, everything will be fine. Ms. Jones isn't going to do anything to you."

"If she damages anything, sir, you're going to have to pay for it."

"I'm not worried about that. Here's the check for the amount you stated." Heather took the check and produced paperwork for me to sign so I would be out of the lease.

"Thank you so much. If there's anything else I need from you, I'll give you a call."

"That's fine. Enjoy the rest of your day, Heather. If Shanell comes back down here starting anymore trouble, *then* you call the police."

"Mr. King, she's crazy. I've never seen her behave in that manner before. I'm scared, and I think she may try to harm me."

"Heather, I guess you better beat her ass the best you can or lock yourself in this office. Call the police and tell them just that. I really don't care if she gets locked up. Shanell is not my responsibility anymore." I shrugged.

Leaving Heather in the office, I made my way back out the door. Dap was sitting back chilling when I got back in the car. He took off and merged into traffic leading the way to our next destination.

"Where are you going, bro?" I asked after sitting back as he drove.

"I want you to come check something out with me and tell me what you think. It's the perfect time since we're already downtown. How did things go back there?"

"Nigga! Shanell showed her natural black ass. She threatened to beat the manger up and started screaming she gon' see me. I'm not worried about her because she just talking. Hopefully she'll be out tomorrow like she stated."

"You better be worried because you gon' have to kill her, straight up. We're talking about a bitch that's obviously dickmatized, and you snatched that shit from under her ass. Shanell is now in the category as a woman scorned, and you can't trend lightly on this situation. There's no telling how she's about to turn your world upside. Everybody closes to you should know what's going on between y'all. That includes Pops and your mama."

"Dap, I'm a grown-ass man and this is my business. Crying to them is weak as fuck!"

"Who said anything about crying? It's beyond that, bro. Shanell don't know where *you* live, but she sure as hell knows where the fuck my daddy lay his head! They have a right to know just in case she decides getting at you or Justice becomes too much of a difficult task."

"You have a point. I didn't think about it like that. Again though, Shanell knows how far to take her stupidity."

"I can't speak on what type of relationship y'all had, but I can say she has been cut the fuck off and her money has been tampered with. She's not walking away quietly, bro. I'd advise you to cancel cards, phones, or whatever she has connecting the two of you together. Sever all ties!" Dap barked as he pulled along the curb. He cut the engine and got out without waiting on a reply from me.

Following his lead, I got out and walked behind him to an empty store next to Garrett's popcorn shop. "Why the hell we at an empty-ass building, bro? All these stores and you come to one that's not even in business," I said, standing beside him confused.

"Remember when I told you about opening Customs by Dap II? This is me, bro. I'm not playing around when it comes to my cheddar. I figured since all the folks with money love to shop on Michigan Avenue, this would be the perfect spot. My designs are a hit in Cali and I'm ready to take over the Chi too," he said, smiling from ear to ear.

I was glad he had something to get the frown off his face. Dap placed a key in the lock and walked inside. The spot was spacious and was in a great spot. There was no way he couldn't strive and do what he did best.

"I'm going strictly with my jewelry at this location. Michigan Avenue isn't the place for my clothing line. I'm going to open another spot somewhere else for that but my vision is clear in my eyes and the spot is empty. The contractors will be coming in to put my plan in motion in a couple months. I'm excited about it."

"That's what's up! I need you to get some security in place because things are different out here now. Shit is not the same as they were when we were growing up."

"Wes, you of all people know, I'm not worried about none of that shit. I'm still the same nigga and wish a muthafucka would. They better come through with some heavy hittas on their team. I got my crew from Cali coming this way when I'm ready for them. I got this."

"I know you can hold your own, bro. I was just giving you a heads up. You got this shit and I'm proud of all you've accomplished."

"Get outta here with all that mushy shit," He laughed. "Nah, but for real, I appreciate that. I've been working on the promotional shit already because the Grand opening is going to be off the muthafuckin' chain."

"I'm here for it, bro! If you need me to help in anyway, let me know."

"No doubt. I'm just glad I could bring this shit back home and make it happen once again. This is just the beginning though. Watch me work. Come on, let's get out of here so we can go see Pops."

We got back to the car just in time because the law had pulled up to ticket Dap's Beemer. Jumping inside, he peeled off soon as both cops opened their doors to step out. His dumb ass laughed all the way to the expressway because he left them in the dust.

Chapter 8
Bria

Shanell had been blowing my phone up since Wes told her she had to vacate the apartment she had been living in. We had been best friends since the day Wes brought her home with him damn near ten years ago. I thought they were going to walk down the aisle together and was shocked when he told me he was married and Shanell wasn't his wife.

The shit pissed me off because Shanell held that nigga down better than his homies in the street on many occasions. When he got locked up and was sentenced to four years in prison, she was right there rocking with his black ass. So, she fucked Curt. What else was she supposed to do when his ass was in a relationship with the Department of Corrections?

I didn't appreciate him turning his back on her the way he was. On top of that, he put his hands on her, and he wasn't raised like that at all. Then he took his wife to the girl's house and thought it was going to be cool when he only repeated what they had already talked about. She's better than me, I swear, because I would've beat both of their asses.

"Mommy, I'm hungry," Sage, my five-year-old son, said, breaking my thoughts.

"Hey, baby. You finally woke up, huh? What do you want to eat?"

"I want Cocoa Pebbles," he said, jumping up and down.

"Alright, let's go downstairs and make it happen then." Sage ran out of my room and I followed close behind him. "What I tell you about running? Walk before you fall down those stairs."

"Okay, Mommy," he said, slowing down as he held on to the banister.

Upon entering the kitchen, I headed straight for the cabinet to get a bowl. Sage sat in one of the chairs at the table and waited patiently as I poured his cereal and added milk. As I walked over to him, I took in his features and sighed loudly because he looked just like his damn daddy. He had the same olive-shaped eyes, dark skin, and fine hair. I had to shake my head because I didn't want to think about his ass at the moment.

"Thank you, Mommy. You not eating with me?" he asked with a mouthful of cereal.

"No, Mommy isn't hungry. Hurry and eat. You have to go to school soon." Sage's school day started at noon, and I welcomed the four hours of time I had to myself when he was gone.

My phone rang and I took it out of the pocket of my robe. It was a Facetime call from Shanell. I closed my eyes and opened them before I answered. "Good morning, chic. What's going on?"

"I'm gon' end up hurting your brother!" she screamed.

"Hold that thought, Sage is sitting right here," I told her so she wouldn't go any further. "We'll talk about it when I drop him off at school.

"Let me talk to my li'l baby," she said cheerfully. I turned the camera around so Shanell could see Sage. "Hey, Tee Tee's baby. How are you doing this morning?"

"I'm good. When you coming here to eat cereal with me?" he asked, smiling.

"Soon, buddy. Soon. How's school going?"

"School is good, but sometimes I don't want to go." Sage pouted.

"Why not? Somebody's bothering you?" I asked, getting mad instantly.

92

"No. Olivia don't want to be my girlfriend. She always talking about her daddy gon' beat me up because he said she can't have a boyfriend. What's wrong with her daddy, Mommy? I'm a good dude!"

I couldn't do anything but laugh because my baby was serious. "Sage, what you know about having a girlfriend?"

"I was watching cartoons on my iPad and a video came on, right? A little boy about my age was saying he had a girlfriend and how much he liked her. He was buying her milk and cookies at school and he was smiling when he talked about her. But when I tried to get Olivia like that, she started talking about what her daddy said. I don't care about her daddy, Mama! She wouldn't even drink the milk I bought her."

"Sage, you're not old enough to have a girlfriend. Wait until you are a little older, baby. Olivia has to listen to what her father tells her. If she is the one for you, she will be there when y'all get older, okay?" I tried to explain to him.

"Mama, she doesn't even want to sit by me at lunch anymore. That hurts my feelings every day. Am I a bad dude?" he asked with tears in his eyes.

"No, there's nothing bad about you. Don't cry, baby. Olivia probably likes you, but as a friend. Give it time; be a kid. All that other stuff will come later when you're older." Shanell said, adding her two cents.

"Okay, Tee Tee. I need y'all to find my daddy because I need him right now to help me with Olivia's daddy. He can't keep me away from my girl," He pouted.

I turned the camera back around so Shanell could see my face and we both shook our heads. "I'll call you back when I drop him off," I said, taking the empty bowl to the sink.

"You better find that boy's daddy, Bria."

"Fuck you, Shanell," I snapped, hanging up on her.

"Mommy, you're not supposed to say bad words," Sage said seriously.

"I know. Mommy's sorry. Go upstairs and put on the clothes I have laid out on your dresser. Sage, don't be up there playing either, we have thirty minutes before we have to leave out. And brush your teeth and wash your face."

His little ass got down out of the chair and ran his ass out of the kitchen. "Sage!" I yelled.

"I know, stop running. I got it, Mommy. Hurry and get dressed. I can't wait to see Olivia," he said, stomping up the stairs.

After washing the bowl and spoon, I made my way upstairs to throw on something quick so I could take Sage to school. It felt good not to punch a clock for work. Setting my own schedule was the way I wanted it to be and I made it happen. My online merchandise store was booming and I was proud of myself.

I thought back to five years ago when I up and left Chicago without telling anyone until I made it to Michigan. My parents thought I was going to visit, but that was far from the truth. I had no intentions of ever returning to live in the city of Chicago.

My father was pissed, but I was twenty-two and there was nothing he could say about it. After a while he realized he had to let me make my own mistakes and he let it go. For the first year, he sent money and helped pay my bills. He even put up the money to get my business started, and I couldn't thank him enough. If anyone in my family found out the real reason I left, all hell would break lose.

"Mommy, I'm ready," Sage said, standing in my doorway with his jacket and bookbag on his back.

"Okay, when I put on my shoes we can go."

"I was looking at TV yesterday and *Toy Story 4* is playing at the movies. Can we go since I don't have school tomorrow? It's Saturday, you know."

"Sage, this isn't the weekend for us to go to the movies. Mommy has to pay the bills." I messed up spoiling him the way I did, but I wouldn't have it any other way.

"Don't worry, I got you this time around. I've been saving the money you give me. Maybe Olivia can come too. I'm paying, so can we go please?"

I smiled and stood after tying my Air Max sneakers then grabbed my jacket. "Yes, Sage, we can go. But I don't think Olivia will be able to go this time around. Maybe next time when Mommy has more money. We're going to make this Mommy and son day, okay?"

"Okayyyy," he pouted.

"Let me find out you love Olivia more than me, Sage," I said with my hand on my hip.

"I don't love her more than you, but she comes in second place for sure. Let's go so I can see my girlfriend."

"This boy is just like his smooth-talking-ass daddy," I said to myself as we made our way downstairs to get in the car.

It took ten minutes to get age to school and he was out of the car before giving me a hug and kiss when he saw Olivia standing in line. I sat in the car until Sage's class disappeared into the building behind their teacher. Before pulling into traffic, I pushed the button to Facetime Shanell back.

"Did you find Sage's daddy?" She asked with a smirk on her face.

"Girl, Sage better keep loving me and forget about that fool. We're not about to talk about that bullshit though. What happened between you and Wes now, Shanell?"

"This muthafucka came to the manager's office at the apartment and terminated the lease! I have to be out by Monday, but I'll be out of this damn place tonight."

"Why would you tell them you will be out by tonight, Shanell? Monday would've given you a window to pack without rushing. You let your emotions fuck you over," I said, glancing down at the screen.

"Bria, I don't care about any of that. I told them tomorrow, but I'm not waiting. I've already booked a hotel room until I can find a place to live. You and I both know money is not an issue for me. One thing I can say is your brother laced my bank account every month. I would've been a fool not to save some of it for a time like this. How long the money will last is another story."

"Don't worry about that. We will deal with it when the time comes. Right now, I want you to get yourself together. I know you're not going to let my brother get away with the bullshit he put you through."

"Hell nawl! He is going to pay for every fuckin' day he wasted my damn time. His wife thinks she has won, but I have news for her. His fuck-up is now hers, and both of them will get what's coming to them. Now I need you to tell me everything I need to know so I can put my plan in motion," Shanell said as she placed items in a box.

Chapter 9
Dap

I pulled into my father's driveway and he was standing at the door before I could turn the engine off. Both Wes and I got out of the car and walked toward the porch.

"Donovan, is that you? What a surprise!"

"Wes G, what's happenin' old man? Stop acting like you miss me." I laughed, walking up the steps.

Pulling me in a tight hug, my father hit me repeatedly on my back. Even though we talked weekly, I knew he truly missed me. There wasn't a day that went by when he wasn't making suggestions for me to come home. Truthfully speaking, he was part of the reason I returned.

"If you ever wait years to bring your ass back, I'll kill you."

"Nah, the wait is over, I'm here to stay. I've bought a crib and everything." I smiled proudly, stepping out of his grasp.

Wes cleared his throat getting our attention. "What the hell, you don't see me standing here?"

"Junior, I see your ass too much! That's the reason I changed my muthafuckin' locks. Come here with your spoiled ass," my father said with his arms outstretched.

"I'm good. Don't use me as an afterthought. I want you to call your long-lost son when Mama wants something reconstructed in this house."

Wes left us standing on the porch and we laughed at his jealousy. It was smelling good when we entered and I knew right away that Beverly was throwing down in the kitchen. Bypassing the living room where Wes went pouting, I made my way to the food.

Beverly was stepping all by her lonesome, but she was getting it. Taking the liberty of moving behind her so she couldn't see me, I started dancing with her. *"I Feel Like Steppin'"* by Alvin Stone was blaring on her Bluetooth speaker and she was in a groove. I grabbed her hand, spinning her out, and when she turned on command, she screamed when she saw it was me.

"Oh my God! Hey, my baby," she said, hugging me. "When did you get in town?" she asked, reaching over to turn the music down.

"I've been here a couple weeks, but don't start fussing. I had a lot to get in order and I've been running nonstop. How have you been?"

"I can't complain. Is my knucklehead son here with you?" she asked, stirring something in a big pot. From the smell alone, I knew it was collard greens, and I wasn't leaving until I had some in my stomach.

"Yeah, he's in there pouting, as usual. Speaking of Wes, there's something he needs to tell you and Dad. Come in the living room to listen so you can get back in here and finish cooking. I'm hungry," I said, rubbing my stomach.

"The food is about done, and you know you're welcome at my house anytime. Now what's going on with my son? He's not back in these streets, is he? If he is, I'm going to bust his head open."

"Nah, nothing like that, I promise. But I'll let him explain everything to y'all," I said, leading the way to the other room.

Beverly always treated me like a son even though my father stepped out on their marriage with my mama. There was never any malice in her when it came to me. If anything, she embraced me and brought Wes and I up as what we were, brothers. I have much respect and love for her, just as I love my biological mother. Nothing can break the bond we have as a family.

Wes and Pops was shooting the breeze as we walked in the room. I took a seat on the loveseat as Beverly sat next to Wes. He leaned in and gave her a kiss on the cheek before wrapping her in his arms.

"Hey, baby. What's going on? Donovan said you wanted to talk to us about something. Everything okay?" she asked, turning slightly toward him.

Wes glared at me, but I didn't give a fuck. He needed to fill them in on what was going on. "Donovan talks too much," he said, shaking his head. "I broke things off with Shanell the other day—"

"Wait a minute!" Beverly shouted, cutting Wes off. "What the hell you mean the other day? Wes, you've been married almost a year. We had a conversation about that shit when you told me you proposed to Justice. I asked you were you still messing with Shanell, and you told me you weren't. What kind of games are you playing?"

Beverly was pissed and she didn't try to hide how she felt. She kept glancing at Pops and he sat quietly until she finished because we all knew she was far from done. Wes was in for a rude awakening, and I kind of felt sorry for him.

"Ma, I'm not playing any games. I'm done with Shanell."

"You should've *been* done with her when she was fucking around on you instead of being there when you were locked up. I wouldn't have expected her to be there for the long haul, but she could've dated someone that wasn't close to you. After that incident, I had no more respect for her ass."

"Beverly, let him talk," Pops said from his recliner.

Wes looked uncomfortable and I thought he wasn't going to continue, but he eventually did.

"Okay, I may have messed up by not ending things with Shanell. Y'all know how she was when she lost the baby with her mental state. I didn't want her to do anything to harm herself, so I did what I thought was the right thing at the time. Things escalated with me and Justice and I didn't know how to cut Shanell off. I was still sleeping with her, but not like we were together."

"You sound dumb as hell! As long as you were still having sex with her, in her mind, you were still her man. I wouldn't be surprised if she started acting crazy," Beverly growled.

"Too late," I muttered, rubbing my head.

"What do you mean too late, Donovan?" my father asked, sitting up.

"I'll tell you," Wes said, standing to his feet. "I terminated the lease on the apartment Shanell and I lived in. I was forced to tell Justice about Shanell because I went to see her and the sun beat me home," Wes explained. Beverly shook her head, but didn't utter a word. "Justice was mad, but she told me to cut everything off with Shanell and forced me to take her to the apartment. While there, Shanell found out Justice was pregnant."

"Son, you were withholding information from both of those women? Shanell should've known Justice was pregnant and you should've told her what kind of relationship y'all had. Honestly is the best policy, son. I'm not saying what you were doing was right, but it's not what you do, it's how you do it."

Pops wasn't wasting anytime spitting a load of truth to Wes. He sat on the sofa looking like a child that was getting scolded. There was nothing I could do for him, because I wasn't trying to get chewed out for something that had nothing to do with me.

"Your wife comes first in your life, and when you fuck up, you never want the truth to come out without being upfront. I see myself in you and I've done my share of dirt, but I've never left your mother in the dark. When I almost lost her was the day I left all the bullshit alone. Justice may not forgive you the way your mother did, so you better pray and do damage control," my father said to Wes.

"Justice left the house and I don't know when she will be back. She hasn't completely cut me out of her life, but she really ain't fucking with me. Shanell, on the other hand, is mad because she's been cut off. She told me to watch myself, but I'm not worried about her."

"Brah, I don't know how many times I have to tell you to stop brushing her ass off. She's gonna be a problem. That's the reason I advised him to come tell y'all what was going on. There's no telling what she would try to do."

"She ain't crazy enough to come here with that mess. I haven't barred her from my home but I will, after I beat her ass. All I'm going to say is get that shit under control because nothing better happens to my grandbaby while yo' ass trying to be a pimp. The shit didn't work for your daddy and Justice don't seem like she's going to take your shit, so fix it!"

Beverly got up and walked into the kitchen still mumbling to yourself. I looked at Wes and he looked defeated. My daddy sat back in his recliner and turned the TV on. "Son, clean up your house. Happy wife, happy life. Need I say more?"

Meesha

Chapter 10
Justice

It had been three weeks since Wes got caught with his hand in the cookie jar. I talked a lot of shit when it happened but deep down, I wanted to divorce his muthafuckin' ass. My heart was damn near torn out of my chest, but I refused to let anyone see me shed a tear over the bullshit. Bedtime was the time I used to get everything off my chest, and Wes calling fifty times a day didn't make things any better.

My mother called one day during the second week and instantly knew from the sound of my voice something was wrong. When I broke down and told her what was going on, she asked me what I wanted to do. Celine Page was not one to sugar coat anything and she didn't start the day she talked to me.

"Justice, I didn't raise you to take shit from nobody. Wes is your husband, and if you want to divorce his ass, I'm standing behind you on your decision. One thing I want you to know is this: you don't ever let a bitch break up your home. Don't get me wrong, Wes played a major part in the fuck-up, but you can handle his ass because you have the upper hand with him. If you leave him, she is going to think she won. Nah, we ain't having that shit. You say you love him, right? Then love his ass, but let him know you are not to be played with. Make him prove he wants to be with you without the fucking games."

The entire conversation played in my mind for an entire week before I decided to go back home. I made my decision based on the fact that my due date was approaching fast and I was afraid of going into labor without him by my side. I went on maternity leave the day after I left to stay at Tana's house. Spending my days inside was something I wasn't used to, but I was making the best of it.

Wes had been buying so many flowers that the damn house was starting to look like a damn funeral home. I was all for getting flowers while I was alive to smell them, but damn, it was too much. He spent a lot of his time getting the nursery ready and I hadn't seen it as of yet because he refused to let me see until the baby was born. I was cool with it because he was putting his heart and soul into whatever he was doing behind the closed door.

It had been quiet and Wes hadn't been getting any of the outrageous calls I thought would come after the manager at the apartment Shanell moved out of called. Shanell trashed the place and we had to pay close to eight thousand dollars for the damage. The shit she did was disgusting and I'd never seen anything like it.

The bitch needed to be in a psychiatric hospital because she smeared feces over all the walls and wrote "Weston King is a dead man walking" in shit. There were blood trails throughout the apartment, every mirror was broken, and she even carved "I love Weston King" in the walls. Shanell was arrested for vandalism but somehow, she was able to get out of jail on bond. I found myself asking Wes if the crazy bitch knew where we lived a hundred times a day. But he swore she didn't know, so I left it alone.

I was sitting in the living room watching the latest episode of *The Masked Singer*. As I sang and danced along with the flower, whom I knew right away was Patti Labelle, a sharp pain in my stomach doubled me over. The baby was twisting and turning like a contortionist and the shit didn't feel good at all. Thinking nothing of it, I continued watching my show until another pain shot up my back fifteen minutes later.

I breathed deeply until the pain started to subside and decided to walk around for a little bit. My due date was a week away, but I wasn't thinking maybe I was in labor. I had a doctor's appointment the next day, so I was going to thug it out until then.

It was three o'clock in the afternoon so I had three hours before Wes would walk through the door. There was a small pot of cabbage, candied yams, baked barbeque chicken, and cornbread already waiting in the kitchen for dinner. Deciding to head upstairs to lay comfortably in my bed, I turned the TV off and climbed the stairs slowly.

I had barely stepped into my bedroom when another sharp pain shot across the middle of my belly. I gripped the edge of the dresser and my knees buckled, causing me to lean over resting my head down. It felt as if my baby was in there doing Pilates as it stretched the length of my stomach and then some. Tears ran down my face as I pounded on the dresser.

Once again, the pain eased up, giving me the opportunity to climb onto the bed. Glancing at the time on my phone, I kept it in mind to see how far apart the pains were. Lying on my side, I logged into my social media account to see what was going on while rubbing my belly. There was a red number one notifying me of an inbox message I had waiting for me.

It was odd because I really didn't have many friends on my page. Tana had suggested I make a profile to keep in touch with old college friends when we used to go on trips and shit. If it was up to me, she could've kept me in the know, but she said it was too much and I may as well make my own. The message was from someone by the name of "Imthatbytchperiod".

Spam was the first thing that came to mind because I didn't associate with anyone that would be proud enough to display themselves in that manner on social media. My first mind was to delete the message, but curiosity led me to open the damn thing. There were about ten pics, but for some odd reason they had to load because I couldn't view them.

Turning the TV on, I went straight to the Investigation Discovery channel. The show *Obsessions: Dark Desires* was on and the episode was one I'd never seen before. The position I was lying in was doing the trick because my baby must've fallen asleep. The show had my attention because there was a guy stalking this woman to the extreme and had her going out of her mind.

My phone chimed and I looked down and saw I had yet another message from the mystery person in my inbox. Picking up my phone, I clicked the app to go in and almost choked on my spit. There was a picture of Wes and Shanell in a compromising position. I scrolled through the pictures and each one was of them having sex.

I knew right away Shanell was the culprit. "I guess this is the moment I'm supposed to get mad." I laughed out loud. The photos were before Wes met me because she forgot to crop the dates out at the bottom. She was quiet for a reason, and the hoe was just getting started. One thing I can honestly say is she better have a plan A, B, and C fucking with me, because I was on whatever her messy ass was on.

As I got to the last picture, I noticed there was a written message underneath. Glancing up at the top of the page, I saw the person was still active, which made me laugh even more because keyboard boxing wasn't something I did in my pastime. I started reading silently and shook my head at every word.

"If you think our husband is going to leave me alone, you are sadly mistaken. I've invested nine years into that nigga and I'll be damned if I give it up just because he married you. Yeah, you talked him into terminating the lease on my place, but he blessed me with another. See, what Wes and I have is

something he would never have with you. In other words, he ain't going nowhere."

This heifer was out of her mind and I didn't have time for her shenanigans. Taking a screenshot of the entire message, I started a new text so I could send it to Wes because I wasn't about to entertain her clown ass. Once I input the pictures in the message box, I typed a note for him.

"Check ya friend before she gets her feelings hurt. I can't stand a social media thug, Wes. I'm too old for the games she's playing. This is the type of shit that happens when you fuck around instead of closing all doors before opening another."

I had no idea how she even found my page because I didn't use my real name. My name on the site is "JustUsP" and I have under fifty people that are friends with me.

Shaking my head, I got out of bed so I could go relieve my bladder with my phone in hand. When I took the first step, my peanut decided to do somersaults like it was part of Jesse White's tumbling team.

"Sssssssss, come on, baby, that hurts," I said out loud as I held on to the side of the bed. I looked at the time on my phone and it had been ten minutes since the last bout of pain subsided. "These can't be contractions. It's not time." I felt like a fool talking to myself but I was low-key scared because I was home alone and it would take Wes too long to get to me.

My phone rang as I walked slowly to the bathroom. I answered as I sat on the toilet, urinating like a damn race horse. "Hello," I said, breathing slowly.

"Baby, you okay?" Wes asked.

"Yeah, this baby is having a party in my damn uterus. I'm alright though. Did you see my message?"

"I got it. Justice, don't feed into that shit. Shanell is trying to get a rise out of you. I didn't help her get another place. You know that. I've given you complete control of my accounts and you can check them anytime you want. She's lying and those pictures are old. Didn't you see the date?"

"Wes, I know the pictures are old and I'm not worried about any of that. I'm trying to figure out how the hell she found me on that damn blue app. I don't even be on there like that."

"Honestly, she probably went through my friend's list and sought you out. I haven't even talked to her, I swear."

Standing up after wiping, I reached back to flush the toilet and a gush of fluid splashed on the floor. "Oh my God, Wes, my water just broke!" I shrieked into the phone.

"You gotta be kidding me, right?"

"No, I'm serious! I've been having pains for the past hour but I ignored them. I have to call Dr. Brown because the baby isn't due until next week. I have an appointment tomorrow morning and I was trying to wait until then."

"Justice, you should've called and told me. I could've been home just in case you needed to go the hospital. Now, I won't make it there for over an hour because rush hour traffic is about to be thick as fuck," he said, panicking.

"I didn't want to worry you if it was a false alarm." Wes didn't say anything after my response. "Wes, you still there?" I asked. The sound of him tapping his fingers on something could be heard then his voice boomed through the phone.

"Bro, I need you to go by the house. Justice's water just broke and I'm at work, but I'm leaving now." He was quiet for a bit before he spoke again. "A'ight cool. Thanks, man, I owe you one. See you at the hospital. Baby, Dap is on his way to pick you up. He should be there in about ten minutes. He isn't too far away."

"Okay, I'll see you soon," I said, stepping over the puddle.

Wes ended the call and I cleaned up the best I could at the sink. Going back into the bedroom, I pulled on a pair of leggings after placing a sanitary napkin in my underwear and donned one of Wes's shirts. Slipping my feet in a pair of black Nike slides, I went to the closet and picked up the bag I had packed a while back. I picked up my phone and texted my doctor. She was probably busy at the hospital, so I figured I might have to wait awhile before she responded.

As I walked down the stairs, my phone rang and I answered it quickly. "Hello."

"Hey, boo. What are you up to?" Tana asked.

"Girl, I'm about to take my fat ass to the hospital. My water broke."

"Yasssss, my baby is ready to get out of that muthafuckin' hot box!" she screamed. "Wes better drive fast but safely."

"Wes is at work. He's going to meet me at the hospital."

"I know damn well you're not driving yourself!"

"No, Donovan is on his way to get me," I said as the doorbell sounded. "As a matter fact, he's here now."

"Well, I was on my way there to surprise you with some Chipotle because we had a half day. I guess I'll see you at the hospital. I'm glad I called when I did."

Peeking out the side window, I saw Wes's brother standing on the other side of the door so I didn't hesitate to open it for him. "You good, sis?" he asked in his deep baritone before reaching out to take the bag from me.

"Damn, he sounds like he's fine as fuck!" Tana screamed in my ear.

"Girl, bye! I'll see you shortly." I laughed as my other line beeped in my ear. "Dr. Brown is calling and I have to answer." I clicked over before she could say anything else. "Hello."

"Justice, is everything okay?"

"My water broke and I'm on my way to the hospital."

"That active baby is ready to show its face, I see. Well, let the party begin. I've been delivering babies since this morning, may as well add you to the list."

"Yeah, may as well. I'll be there soon. Thanks for always being there, Doc."

"That's what I'm here for. Now get here! I'm excited about this one," she said, hanging up.

"Sorry about that. I'm ready," I said to Donovan as I set the alarm.

"No problem. Are you in any pain?"

"Not at the moment, but I can't wait to get to the hospital where the drugs are," I said, laughing nervously.

"You got this, Justice. There's nothing to be scared about," he said, holding on to my arm as we walked down the steps to his car.

Chapter 11
Tana

It took me a good ten minutes to get to South Suburban Hospital in Hazel Crest. After entering through the automatic doors, I approached the counter to find out where Justice was.

"Welcome to South Suburban, how may I help you?" the young lady greeted me.

"Justice King was brought in because her water broke. Would you tell me where she is?"

"Okay, let me see what we have here," she said, typing away on the keyboard.

As I waited, the doors to the hospital opened and Justice's voice bellowed out behind me. "Tana, how did you beat me here?"

Turning around, I instantly saw the discomfort on my friend's face. "Thank you, ma'am, I found her," I said to the woman behind the counter. "Actually, you can get her admitted into the system though. Her name is Justice King and her doctor, Elizabeth Brown, is waiting for her."

"Okay, I have that information in front of me. I'll page Dr. Brown and you guys should be on your way in no time. Congratulations on your bundle, Mrs. King."

"Thank you," Justice replied, grimacing as she rubbed her stomach.

"Are you in pain, Just?" I asked.

"Yeah, I think I need to sit down."

The fine-ass man that walked in with Justice walked across the lobby and grabbed a wheelchair. "Sit down, sis. It will be over soon."

"Thanks, Donovan," Justice said as Dr. Brown graced us with her presence.

"Well hello, my favorite mommy-to-be. Thank you, Sheryl, I'll take it from here," Dr. Brown said to the receptionist. "I already have a room ready for you. Follow me."

I glanced at Donovan and he looked very concerned as he pushed Justice toward the elevator. The car was quiet as we rode up, but I continued to steal glances at Justice's brother-in-law on the low. His caramel complexion was smooth and he had a pair of sexy dimples in each cheek. I envisioned myself lying back on his chest stroking his goatee while he played with my kitty.

"Baby girl, you getting off?" Donovan asked as he held the door open to the elevator.

"Oh, yeah. My mind was somewhere else," I said, stepping off. My face was warm as hell because I had been caught lusting over someone I knew nothing about. Donovan led the way to the room Justice was assigned to and we were asked to stay out in the hall until she was situated.

"You guys can sit over there and I'll let you know when she's ready," a nurse said as she sat behind the nursing station.

My phone chimed with a text as I sat down and I sighed when Tyson's name displayed on the screen.

"Let it go, shawty. Stress kills and causes wrinkles to form on ya face," Donovan said out of nowhere.

I chuckled because I was debating if I should reply to Tyson or not before Donovan's voice interrupted my thoughts once again. "I've let it go, but I don't think he received the memo. I'm about to cuss him out for the last time and maybe he will leave me alone."

"Nah, you doing too much. Stop giving him attention. That will be enough. The more you feed into his bullshit, the more he will feel you care," Donovan said, taking my phone.

"You don't even know me to be taking my phone. Give it back."

"Well, since we have time, I'm Donovan. And you are?" he said, revealing his sexy ass dimples.

"I am, give me my damn phone." I laughed.

"You're not getting this phone until you tell me your name and relationship to Justice."

"I'm Tana, and the auntie to the baby that's eager to enter this dreadful world we live. I've known Wes since he's been with my friend and never knew he had a brother."

Before he could respond, his phone rang and he answered. "Hey, Bria. It's been a minute, what's going on?" He paused. "Cool, cool. I'm at South Suburban waiting on Wes because Justice went into labor," he said, pausing again. "Aight, you should give him a call and congratulate him yourself. I hope you come home soon. I would love to see you."

I don't know what happened after that, but he hung up rapidly with a look of confusion on his face. Doctors and nurses flooded into Justice's room and closed the door. When I rose from my seat to see what was going on, the door opened and Justice was being wheeled down the hall at a fast pace.

"What's going on?" I asked one of the nurses.

"The baby's heart rate is very low. Dr. Brown wants to do an emergency cesarean to deliver the baby. Is Mr. King here to accompany her in the OR?"

"I'm here!" Wes yelled out, rounding the corner.

"Okay, we need you immediately with your wife," the nurse explained, rushing Wes down the hall.

I got comfortable in my seat and once again, it was just me and Mr. Sexy alone waiting. I prayed in silence for Justice to have a safe delivery for her and the baby. Playing a cooking game on my phone to pass time, I zoned everything around me out. Not knowing how much time passed, I heard Donovan mutter under his breath and glanced up from my phone.

There was a woman gliding down the hall towards us with a smirk on her face. Donovan's mouth was curled in a snarl. She had on a pink jogging suit with a pair of pink and white sneakers and her hair was in a ponytail that sat high on top of her head. I got a bad vibe from her and she hadn't even reached us to open her mouth. Slipping my phone into my purse, I sat up as the woman stood in front of Donovan.

"How the fuck did you know to come here?" he asked, leaning forward on his knees.

"I have my ways, brother," the unknown woman chuckled. "Where is Wes?" At that moment, I knew exactly who the bitch was and I wanted her to get out of pocket so I could fuck her up.

"Shanell, I'm not your brother. I have never addressed you as my sister and won't start now. Again, how did you know we were here? I won't continue to repeat myself."

"That's not important. All I want to do is talk to Wes."

"You won't get the chance, so just leave. This is a family matter, and the last time I checked, you weren't family." Donovan rose to his feet and folded his arms over his chest. Shanell's eyes landed on me, then back up to Donovan.

"Dap, you still don't scare me, nigga—"

"Shanell!" Her head turned in the direction she heard her name being called and she groaned in frustration. "I know damn well you didn't come to this hospital being messy," a short petite woman said, rushing toward us.

"Beverly, all I want to do is talk to Wes."

"Leave before I have security to force you to leave. This don't make any sense. My son cut all ties with you and you're still chasing behind him. It's over, Shanell."

"Where were y'all when I lost my baby? None of y'all was with me but now that his *wife* is having a baby, it's one big family reunion!" Shanell snapped. "I see it was fuck me then and it's fuck me now!"

"Lower your voice when you're talking to my wife. You will not disrespect her because you're in your feelings. Don't try to throw losing the baby in our faces because that guilt shit only worked with my son. If you had called, we would've been there for you. No questions asked." The guy I assumed was Wes's father scolded Shanell like she was his child, but she didn't back down.

"It wasn't your job to be there for me! Your son should've been the one by my side like he's back there with his bitch!"

"Shanell, leave this hospital now!" Beverly snarled. "And stay the fuck away from my son."

Shanell walked around Wes's parents and headed down the hall. "Tell your son it ain't over until I say it's over. If he knows what's good for him, he'll answer my calls," she said, disappearing around the corner.

"We gon' have to kill that bitch. She's crazier than a bitsy bug," Donovan said, sitting down while looking down the hall.

"What is Wes saying about this whole Shanell situation?" his dad asked.

"He doesn't think she's going to be a problem, but I beg to differ. As you can see, she is being real stalkerish right now."

His father shook his head and turned toward me. "I'm sorry, I'm Weston Senior, and you are?" he asked with a smile.

"I'm Tana, Justice's best friend Nice to meet you."

"I'm sorry you had to witness that. This is my wife Beverly."

Wes's mom walked over and hugged me tightly. "I hope you know how to fight, because you and Justice is going to end up beating her dumb ass."

I couldn't help laughing, because from what I had just witnessed, I knew she was right. Weston Senior glared at his wife and she hunched her shoulders as she took a seat next to me.

After a while, Wes came pimping down the hall with a huge smile on his face. "I didn't expect for y'all to come out this way," he said to his parents.

"You should've known your mama was going to be here. How's Justice?"

"I'm a daddy, y'all! She had a baby girl and she look just like her mama. She's beautiful." Congratulations were given to Wes and he started handing the men cigars.

"What's her name?" I asked excitedly.

"Faith Marie King. She weighed in at eight pounds and she's twenty inches long with a head full of hair. Mom, I had to give her your middle name because you mean so much to me."

"Awwww, that's so sweet of you, baby. Did you take any pictures?"

"No. Justice will be moved to a room soon and y'all would be able to go in to see her."

Miss Beverly cleared her throat and looked at Donovan, then nodded her head at Wes. I knew she was trying to get him to tell his brother about Shanell popping up and causing a scene. Donovan shook his head no, refusing to say anything. Since no one was going to step up and tell him, I took the liberty to do the honors for them.

"Wes, your friend Shanell came here showing out. You may take her threats lightly, but I won't. If anything happens to Justice behind her delusional ass, I'm blaming you."

"Wait, how did she know we were here? Did one of y'all mention it to her by mistake or something?"

"Wes, we don't fuck with her—" Donovan said and stopped mid-sentence. "Pops, I'm fuckin' your daughter up!"

"What the hell Bria have to do with this? She's all the way in another state."

"I talked to her and mentioned my whereabouts and her ass must've hung up and called Shanell. She's the only one that could've told her what hospital we were at." Donovan took his phone out and pressed a button before putting the phone to his ear.

"Why the fuck would you tell Shanell to come to this hospital? Huh, Bria? Bria?" He looked down at the phone and pushed the button again. "I'm slapping her ass whenever I see her. She did the shit because she hung up and now she won't answer her phone."

"I'll have a talk with Bria soon as we leave here. That don't make any sense for her to initiate this mess," Weston Senior said. "Wes, I think you need to stay away from that woman, cut all contact. That means phone calls and all. She is bad news."

"Dad, I haven't talked to her since I paid the money to terminate the lease. I haven't thought about Shanell. It's all about me, Justice, and Faith from this moment on. Shanell was a mistake I should've left alone a long time ago."

"I hope so," Miss Beverly said, rolling her eyes. "Let's go see my grandbaby. I'm tired of talking about that crazy bitch."

Meesha

Chapter 12
Shanell

If those muthafuckas thought I was going to just go away, they were in for a rude awakening. Shanell wasn't ever going to be silenced by anyone. I was back in another crib three days after Wes terminated the lease. When I got the call that wifey was in labor, I got there soon as I could. It pissed me off when I saw his whole family in that bitch like she was the Queen of Sheba.

So what, I didn't tell them I miscarried. But they didn't call to check up on me either. Now this hoe gets all of their attention because she is actually having a baby. Dap's punk ass even came into town for the occasion, and he hadn't been home in forever. They could smile now, but every last one of them will be crying later if I had anything to do with it.

Leaving the hospital after I was forced out, I went down the street to Starbucks and grabbed a cup of Caramel Brulée Frappuccino. My mind was racing and I got madder by the minute as I waited on my order. After a while my name was called and I stalked out of the establishment and jumped back in my car. Finding myself at Target, I went inside and picked out a lot of neutral baby clothes and a car seat. As I walked toward checkout, Curt was walking down the aisle toward me.

I tried to walk past him but he grabbed me by the arm and glared down at me. "What the fuck is this?" he asked, motioning toward the cart.

"Nigga, didn't you learn from the last time you put yo' hands on me? Give me fifty feet and mind ya business," I said, snatching away.

"You pregnant, Shanell?"

I almost laughed at his goofy ass, but I decided to play with his ass. I needed somebody to keep my pockets fat and a small lie wouldn't hurt. "Nah, now move out of my way, Curt. If I was, I wouldn't need yo' ass to help me anyway."

"Put yo' pride aside and let me take care of my responsibility. Stop acting like a little-ass kid. I forgive you for the shit you did to me. What I did was wrong and I apologize, Shanell."

Standing with my head down, I sniffled and forced a few tears out of my eyes before I looked up at him. "You really crossed the line when you choked me and shoved me into the cabinet. Just go back to your woman, Curt. I'll manage on my own." I cried openly, but was laughing my ass off on the inside.

"Don't cry. I got you, Shanell. I came by the apartment, but was told you didn't live there anymore. That nigga really put you out, huh?"

"Yeah, I live in a shelter but I'll be back on my feet soon. I've been on my own before and survived. I don't need anybody."

"Everybody needs someone and I got you. I can't have you staying in no damn shelter. Meet me at my job tomorrow and I will have some money for you to get a place. I called your phone too and it said the number wasn't in service, is it off?"

"Somebody in the shelter stole my phone and most of my belongings. I don't have enough money to get it turned back on," I lied.

Curt looked down at all the shit I had in the cart and tilted his head to the side. Shit, I forgot I had a cart full of baby items, but I was ready for his ass if he questioned it. Sure enough, I read his mind and he said what I expected him to.

"How don't you have enough money, but you have a cart full of shit you were about to pay for?"

Lowering my voice, I looked up at him and without a second thought I said, "I was going to walk right out here with

Paid in Karma

this shit. You know what I'm capable of. If I don't have it, I make a way. Going without isn't an option for me."

"Shanell, you don't need to be getting in trouble while you're carrying my baby. Leave this shit here and we'll get whatever you want when you get a place. Until then, go get a phone. Hit me up when you get it setup and wait for my call," he said, peeling hundreds off the knot he pulled out of his pocket.

Nodding my head yes, I thought of other ways of getting more money from his gullible ass and formulated a plan of really getting pregnant by his ass. Curt kissed me on the cheek and walked away. I told the salesperson to hold my cart because I left my wallet in my car. As I walked out of the store, just as I thought, Curt was sitting in his ride trying to see what I came out with.

To throw him off, I drove down the street and doubled back to purchase the items with the money he had gave me. I got home in less than ten minutes and put everything in the closet of my spare bedroom. As I walked into the living room my phone rang and it was Wes.

"Hey, baby," I sang into the phone.

"Stop playing yourself, Shanell. Why the fuck was you at the hospital and how did you know I'd be there?"

"Damn, baby, you wouldn't answer my calls so I had to come see you in person. It doesn't matter how I found out your location. Plus, I wanted to congratulate y'all on the baby."

"We both know yo' ass big mad that I have a baby. Quit with the bullshit and stay the fuck away from my family! Once I find out how you're tracking my moves, I'm gon' break ya fuckin' neck, bitch."

Wes was furious, but none of that scared me. He had to come harder than that to stop me from fuckin' him up.

"It's not that easy, Wes. You don't mean what you're saying no way, that's your wife talking. This pussy will always have you coming back where you belong," I purred.

"Keep your twat over there with you. I have no desire to lay down with you ever again."

"That's what your mouth says, nigga. You will not live happily ever after long as I'm not in the picture. See, you fucked over the wrong bitch. You said you would always be there for me and you lied!" I yelled.

"I'm not trying to hear any of the shit you're talking. Don't contact my wife again. We are done and there's nothing more for us to communicate about. Take your medicine, Shanell. That's the only reason you're acting this way."

"Wes, you don't want to see the bad side of me. Please don't make me hurt you," I pleaded, giving him the chance to right his wrong.

"Bye, Shanell," he said, ending the call.

"Wes! Wes! You muthafucka!" I screamed, throwing my phone onto the couch.

I grabbed a vase off the glass table and threw it hard against the wall. Glass shattered in every direction as I fell to my knees, sobbing like a baby. Without a second thought, I picked up a piece of the glass and sliced the palm of my hand. As I watched the blood ooze through my fingers, I began to calm down. Standing to my feet, I walked over to the mantle and smeared the blood across Wes's face on a picture we took together.

"You're going to wish you were dead when I finish with you!" I whispered, slamming the frame face down on the floor.

I went into the bathroom and cleaned the cut on my hand the best I could and wrapped gauze around it. The blood was slowly seeping through the bandage, but that didn't stop me from grabbing my keys and leaving the house. Someone was going to get hurt, and it wasn't going to be me.

***

Entering the hospital, I knew Wes wasn't expecting me to show up after he demanded I stayed away. He of all people knew I wasn't working with a full deck, but he still wanted to push me to the point of no return. There was no one at the front desk, so I made my way to the elevators quick as possible and went up to the Labor and Delivery floor. When I stepped out of the elevator, it was quiet as hell because it was after visiting hours.

I passed a door that read "Staff Only" and tried my luck to see if it was unlocked. To my surprise, it was. My initial thought was to go in and find material to doctor on my hand but a pair of scrubs caught my eyes. Blending in with the other nurses was a great ploy to keep eyes off me as I walked through the halls to find wifey, so my plans changed immediately.

As I slipped the scrubs over my leggings and T-shirt, I exited the room and boldly walked to the nurse's station. God surely was watching over me because once again, there was no one on the payroll doing their jobs. "These muthafuckas are making this too easy for me," I said to myself as I scanned the board for Justice's name.

My eyes landed on her name and she was in room 928. I was about to walk away when I noticed the baby's name beside hers and almost lost it. Faith was the name Wes and I agreed to name our baby if it was a girl. How dare he use it for a baby he had with another bitch! Wes was digging himself into a deeper hole when it came to the shit he was constantly doing to me.

Moving slowly down the dimly lit hall, I watched the numbers on the wall until I was standing outside of room 928. The sound of a baby crying could be heard, but I didn't hear any movement on the other side of the door. I waited a couple minutes before I pushed the door open and entered. Justice was sleeping soundly while the baby cried her little heart out.

There was a bottle on the table, I picked it up and walked over towards the baby bed, standing there for a few seconds before lifting Faith's tiny body into my arms. I fed her the warm milk and burped her afterwards. I even changed her diaper then rocked her back to sleep. All while her mammy slept.

The feeling of having a baby in my arms brought back all the emotions I had of my baby. Faith was beautiful even though she looked like Justice. The longing to hold my own child brought tears to my eyes and I couldn't hold them back. I kissed her on the top of her head before placing her back in the bed and rolled it out of the room without anyone seeing me. Not even Justice.

Chapter 13
Wes

Sitting in the chair beside her bed, I noticed Faith's bed was gone and decided to go out and tell the nurse to bring her back in the room. The nurse Raven was behind the counter tapping away on the keyboard when I approached the counter and looked up immediately.

"Mr. King, how can I help you?" Raven asked.

"I'm missing my princess. Would you have someone bring her to the room please?"

The puzzled expression on her face concerned me. I didn't want to assume anything was wrong, but the uneasy feeling in my stomach told me differently. Raven scanned the chart in front of her and frowned.

"I'm going to the nursery. Wait in the room and I'll be right back," she said, standing abruptly to her feet.

"Is everything okay?" I asked following her down the hall.

"The last log states baby Faith was in the room with your wife. I have to check and be sure she's safely in the nursery before jumping to conclusions. I'm sure everything is fine because if it wasn't, the alarms would've sounded the minute she was removed from the unit."

"Yes, she was in the room with Justice when I left. But now she's not!" I said louder than intended.

"Mr. King, calm down. I'll be back."

Raven rushed down the hall toward the nursery and I headed back in the other direction. My heart was beating rapidly in my chest as I entered Justice's room. The first place I went was to the bathroom to see if Faith was there, but she wasn't. Justice stirred in her sleep and I took that moment to shake her awake.

"Baby, I need you to wake up," I said urgently. "Justice, wake up!"

"Ugh, what is it, Wes?" she asked groggily as she opened her eyes.

"Do you remember when and who took Faith from the room?" I asked, trying not to show any signs of panic.

"Faith is right over there." She pointed to the side of the bed by the window. "What's going on, Wes?" Not wanting to scare her, I slowly sat next to her on the bed and held her hand.

"When I returned from getting your soup, I noticed the baby wasn't here anymore. I went to ask the nurse to bring her back for the night, the log sheet indicated Faith should've still been in here with you. I need you to think. Who came in this room, Justice?"

"I don't know! The nurse gave me medication and I was out for the count. Faith was sleeping in the baby bed. That much I do remember."

I'd heard about people kidnapping newborns from hospitals but hell, I didn't think the shit could happen to us. Justice was fighting to stay awake as tears flowed down her face. All of a sudden, alarms sounded in the hallway and my heart dropped. Jumping to my feet, I dashed for the door.

"Find my baby, Wes," Justice sobbed as her head fell back onto the pillow.

I opened the door. The hall was well-lit and there were security guards, nurses, and doctors scrambling around checking every closed door. I spotted Raven rushing down the hall with tears running down her face. When she noticed me, she stopped and her head dropped to her chest.

"Faith wasn't in the nursery, was she?" I asked, already knowing what her response would be.

"No. I promise I don't know how this could've happened. The only time I left was when I went to the bathroom," she cried.

"I'll help look around. She has to still be here if you said the alarms didn't sound. We have to check everywhere on this floor. Lead the way. I'll follow you. I can't go back in that room without our baby. It will crush my wife."

Raven and I searched the west wing of the building and came up empty. We checked occupied rooms, empty rooms, linen closets, utility closets, stairways, and the bathrooms. Once that part of the building was cleared, we headed to the next one. As we continue to check every nook and cranny, we heard a voice come over one of the security guard's radio.

"We found her! We found the baby! She's in the East wing and her ankle band says Faith King!"

I looked at Raven and she took off running and I was right behind her. When we arrived on the East wing, there was a crowd standing around the baby bed. I pushed my way through and prayed the entire time because the guard never said my baby was okay. A doctor was examining Faith when I was able to lay eyes on her and I let out the breath I'd been holding.

"Where was she found?" I asked no one in particular.

"She was in that linen closet sleeping," one of the guards said, pointing behind him. "The real question is, who would leave a baby in a closet?"

I didn't respond because I wanted to be sure she wasn't hurt. Faith was lying on her back with her doe eyes wide open. Placing my finger in the palm of her little hand, she smiled and held on to it. The doctor looked up at me with a grim expression and let out a deep sigh.

"Mr. King, I don't have an explanation for any of this and on behalf of the staff, I am truly sorry. Faith isn't hurt in any way and I promise to get to the bottom of this."

"Are there any cameras you can view to see who took it upon themselves to play this sick game with *my* baby?"

"Unfortunately, there aren't any cameras. It was after hours and I can't begin to tell you what took place. The police are on the way and I wouldn't blame you for pressing charges against me and the hospital," the doctor said. "Raven, I would like to speak with you in my office. Samantha, escort baby Faith and Mr. King back to their room please. I'll come back to the room to talk to you Mr. King."

"That's fine, but I don't want Nurse Raven to be held accountable for this. She has been nothing short of excellent when it comes to my family. It's not her fault at all. There's no need for her to get in trouble for something an evil person decided to do," I said to the doctor.

"I have to follow protocol, Mr. King. But I will take what you have said into consideration."

The doctor and Raven walked down the hall of the East wing and disappeared around the corner. Nurse Samantha rolled Faith back to the room and I was there beside her. My phone vibrated in my pocket and I pulled it out. There was a text message from an unknown number and I almost ignored it. But something told me to open it.

(312) 555-0523: Now you see that I can touch everything you love. Did your heart drop to your feet when you couldn't find Faith? Yeah, that's the feeling I've had for weeks. This is just the beginning. Get ready to die from the inside out.

I immediately dialed the number and the automated voice stated the phone was no longer in service. Shanell was the only person that came to mind and I couldn't believe she would stoop so low and fuck with my child. As we neared the room,

I took several deep breathes and looked down at Faith. I thanked God for keeping her safe because Shanell could've done more to get back at me.

Justice eyes snapped open when I opened the door. "You found her! Oh my God, my baby is safe," she wailed. "Where was she?"

I turned to Samantha, "Thank you so much for your help. If I need anything, I'll let one of you know." After the door closed behind the nurse, I removed Faith from the bed and laid her upon Justice's chest and sat down. "She was found in a linen closet on the other side of the building."

"How the hell—" she started to ask before I cut her off.

"It was Shanell. Someone left me a text as I was walking back to the room. The text basically taunted me on how I felt when discovering Faith missing. The person also said that's how they've been feeling the last couple weeks. It has to be Shanell, She's the only one that has a problem with me."

"You better find her ass before I do, Wes. I have six weeks to heal, and that gives her the time to do everything she has planned within that time frame because when I catch up with her, I'm going to kill her. That's on everything I love. Your side bitch fucked up when she involved my child in her bullshit."

"Justice you don't have to worry about any of that. Catching a case isn't what you want or you need at this point in life. The police will be here to talk with us and we will allow them to deal with Shanell. I'll show them the text and allow them to take it from there. We have Faith to raise, baby."

Justice stared at me as if I was a stranger. She was still sluggish from the medicine that was in her system, but it didn't stop her from sitting up in the bed with no problem. I opened my mouth to tell her not to worry and she held her hand up and shook her head.

"Did I hear you correctly? Since when a muthafucka from the streets start trusting the police to do their job? Where I come from, we don't do that shit." Justice was mad, but she would eventually get over it because I was doing what was right.

Before I could respond to what she said, there was a tap on the door and two officers entered the room.

"Mr. and Mrs. King, I'm Officer Peterson and this is my partner, Officer Smalls. Sorry to barge in on you all so late, but I want to get your side of the events that took place tonight."

"No problem. I really don't know much about what happened other than I left to get food leaving my wife and daughter here and upon my return, my daughter was nowhere to be found."

"Would you like to make a complaint against the hospital and the nurse that was on duty?" Officer Smalls asked.

Looking over my shoulder at Justice, she had the biggest scowl on her face and I knew she was going to chew me out for my actions. "That won't be necessary. I believe I know who's responsible for this," I said, turning my head toward the officers pulling my phone from my pocket. "I received a text from an unknown number after Faith was found. I believe it's from my ex."

Officer Peterson took my phone and read the text and asked, "What's the name of the person you suspect, Mr. King?"

"Shanell Jones."

"Where can we find Miss Jones and is this her number?" he asked.

"I don't know where she is at this time. I haven't had any contact with her since I broke all ties with her. She has been harassing my wife and now she has played a dangerous game with my daughter. Earlier today she showed up here at the hospital and my family told her to leave. I'm trying to do what's right and not handle things on my own."

Officer Peterson handed my phone back and removed a small notepad from his pocket. "Unfortunately, Mr. King, you don't have solid proof that Miss Jones is responsible for what happened tonight. As far as the text, I wouldn't be able to pinpoint where it was sent from until I run the number through the system," he explained as he wrote on the pad. "What's the best number to contact you, Sir?"

"(708) 555-0711," I recited my cell number.

"Okay, I will get back in touch with you once we find out anything. You guys get some rest and I'm glad there was a happy outcome and baby Faith is alright," Officer Smalls said, turning to open the door.

Justice didn't like the way the officers handled the situation at all. Shifting Faith from her chest to the bed beside her, she sat up straight and folded her arms. Before they could exit the room, she exploded.

"That's it? This bitch took my baby and left her in a closet, texted my husband basically telling him she did it, and y'all blowing the shit off like it's nothing! Y'all would be ready to lock my ass up if I beat the shit out of her. I want to press charges against her right now!"

"Justice, cut it out!" I snapped.

"Fuck that, Wes! Your little friend crossed the line! I'm a mother before anything now. I'm letting y'all know that I'm protecting mine by any means necessary. Shanell don't take rejection well and this is not the end of her bullshit. Y'all can sweep this shit under the rug if you want, but I promise if she keeps coming for me and mine, the next time you see me, it will be to arrest me."

"Mrs. King, we can't allow you to press charges on a person based on speculation. We need for sure evidence, and you don't have that at this time. All I can suggest is for you to document every incident from here on out."

"So you didn't hear anything I said, right? Instead, you're telling us to play ring around the rosy until someone gets hurt before you're willing to do your job, correct? Okay, I understand, but I don't want to hear shit when I'm the bitch doing the hurting. You can leave now. You've said all I needed to hear," Justice said, picking the baby up.

"Mrs.—"

"Just get out! According to you, there's nothing more to be done. Your service is no longer needed, Mr. Officer," Justice snapped, cutting Officer Smalls off.

Bidding farewell, the officers left silently. I looked at my wife in disbelief and she was truly unbothered. Since learning of my relationship with Shanell, Justice's true colors had emerged. The woman I married was quiet and sweet. I didn't know the person lying in the hospital bed holding my daughter.

Chapter 14
Justice

We were released from the hospital after being there four days, and everything was going very well. Faith was calling the shots in our household and I loved every bit of it. At two months, she was almost fourteen pounds and didn't show any signs of slowing down anytime soon. She was such a happy baby and I was glad because one thing I tried not to do was spoil her. Wes was another story in that department. He always had her in his arms, even if she was sleeping.

Wes went back to work two days after I was released from the hospital. He wanted to take two weeks off, but I couldn't stand him smothering me every minute of the day. I insisted he asked his mother to come help out while he worked and he agreed. Beverly and I got along very well and got to know each other in the process.

Shanell had disappeared and no one had heard anything from her. It was in her best interest to stay away for her own good. I meant everything I said to the police and my husband knew that. We even had a conversation about my past in which I didn't hide anything.

Back in the day I did some things I'm not so proud of, but it molded me into the woman I was in the present day. I sold drugs, gang banged, and anything else that was required within the gang I represented. Graduating high school and going away to college saved me from a life of crime, but it didn't erase the hard interior I built during that time. I'd grown, but deep down, my ruthless persona was still there.

When Shanell took it upon herself to hide my baby, my guard went up and the street side of me emerged. Wes couldn't believe some of the things I told him about my past, but it was my life and I told him the truth. My word wasn't good enough, so when Tana came over one day, he needed validation from her and was shocked all over again.

"Justice, I cooked breakfast. Are you coming down?" Beverly asked from the doorway.

"Yes, ma'am," I said, coming out of the bathroom.

"Stop calling me ma'am, chile. I would prefer you call me Mama instead of that shit. I'm not that damn old yet."

I laughed because I knew Beverly hated when I called her ma'am. One day I would be comfortable enough to call her Mama, but I hadn't gotten to that point as of yet. The only person I called Mama was my own.

"I'll be down soon as I slip on some clothes. What did you cook?" I asked.

"You have to come down and see for yourself. Hurry before it gets cold and before my granddaughter decides to wake up," Beverly said, leaving the doorway.

I quickly slipped on a pair of jeans and my Married to Tha Pen T-shirt, put on my slippers, and headed downstairs. Detouring to the guest room Beverly used, I checked in on Faith. My baby was sleeping so peacefully in the middle of the king-sized bed with her little arm covering her face. Smiling, I made my way to the kitchen to devour the food Beverly cooked.

When I entered the kitchen, there was French toast, turkey bacon, eggs, grits, and a glass of orange juice waiting for me on the table. My mother-in-law was eating slowly as I sat down, reaching for the maple syrup. After cutting my French toast, I said a quick prayer and dug in.

"When are you going back to work?" Beverly asked.

"I'm not due to return for another month, but I can't take being at home all day anymore. It's so boring," I groaned. "I called my boss and told him I'd be back next week Monday. I have to look into daycares for Faith."

"Daycare?" Beverly asked, placing her fork down on the plate. "Justice, I don't mind caring for Faith while you and Wes work. I don't trust strangers with my grandbaby, especially since she can't talk. Too much is happening to children in daycares nowadays. Nope, I'm not having that." Beverly shook her head no repeatedly.

"Beverly, you have raised your children. You should be enjoying life," I said, putting eggs in my mouth.

"Baby, you have blessed me with my first grandchild, and there's nothing else I'd rather do than watch her grow. As long as you and Wes are doing something constructive, it's not a problem. It's settled. You can drop Faith off at the house before you head to work."

"Thank you so much. I really appreciate you and Wes Senior helping me through this. It's been tough, but you've taught me a lot about being a mother, as well as my own mama from afar. She would've been here had she not had surgery on her hip. Her coaching via video chat and yours up close and in person prevented me from spazzing out."

"I'll always be here for you. There's no need to thank me. Where does your parents live?"

"They're originally from here, but they relocated to Arizona when I left for college."

We both fell silent as we finished our breakfast and my thoughts were on my parents. Scheduling a visit was a must before I went back to work.

Beverly and I were able to clean the kitchen and relax awhile before Faith decided to join the party. Her soft cries flowed through the baby monitor that sat on the coffee table and I got up so I could tend to her.

After feeding her and changing her diaper, I returned to the living room and sat in the recliner across from Beverly.

Faith was cooing happily as she played with the diamond pendant hanging from the platinum chain around my neck. When she tried to put it in her mouth, I pried it from her hand, and that's when the fight started. That was the first time she cried real tears, and it tugged at my heart.

"Don't you dare cry. She won't be able to get her way all the time. Teach her right from wrong early on and you won't have to worry about it getting out of hand later," Beverly said.

My phone chimed and I leaned over to get it from the table. There was a message in my inbox and when I opened it, the only thing I could do was frown. Shanell was back to her bullshit after being quiet for months. I blocked the other account she made to contact me the first time, and the crazy bitch made another one.

Imthatbytchperiod2: Heyyyy boo! You missed me? I know you didn't think I was going to stay away forever, did you? I have a lot of fun things planned for us, so I hope you're ready. My adventure at the hospital was just the beginning. Shit will definitely be better this time around. I may just harm someone for the hell of it. Oh, tell our man I said hello and I miss that dick.

"Justice, what's the matter?" Beverly asked.

Reading the message again before answering, I shook my head and handed her the phone. Beverly's expression turned from concern to anger in two point five seconds. "I told my son to leave that girl alone years ago. She always gave off bad vibes when she was around. Wes had to learn the hard way, and I'm sorry you are being put in the middle of this madness," Beverly said, shaking her head as she stared at my phone.

"My son was wrong for still messing around with Shanell after he put a ring on your finger. He is lucky you didn't walk away and say fuck him. Believe me, I understand why you didn't ask for a divorce because I had to make a similar decision with Wes Senior. One thing's for certain, don't let this bitch disrupt your family. She's going to slip up, and you better pounce."

Beverly handed my phone back and I took a screenshot of the message, then blocked the account. Glancing down at Faith, I knew in my mind Shanell was on the verge of taking me back to the street life I made a vow to leave in my past. Wes keeps saying she had an illness, but I wasn't trying to hear any of it. Shanell knew exactly what she was doing, and there were no excuses for the things she was doing.

The doorbell rang and Beverly got up to see who was at the door. I heard her thank someone and close the door. She came back with a box and sat it on the table. There was a card attached and I reached over to read it. The card simply said, "To Faith, I love you", which brought a smile to my face.

Handing the baby over to Beverly, I untied the ribbon on the box and lifted the lid. My voice caught in my throat when I saw what was lying inside. There was a newborn baby doll that looked like Faith. She had on the exact sleeper Faith wore the night she was found in the closet at the hospital. There was a kitchen knife lodged in the doll's chest and it had fake blood oozing out of the wound.

Beverly leaned forward and inhaled her breath. "What the fuck is that?" she exclaimed, holding Faith tightly against her chest.

I reached inside the box and grabbed a folded piece of paper that was tucked under the doll's head. My fingers shook as I tried to unfold the paper and it fluttered to the floor. Retrieving it, I opened it and started to read what was written inside.

"Read it out loud," Beverly said, interrupting me.

As you can see, neither of you are untouchable. Now you will be scared to close your eyes at night because you never know when I'll come for my Faith. If I wanted to, I could've stabbed her in the chest at the hospital with a pair of scissors, but I didn't. That don't mean I won't. Hahahahaha! Sweet dreams, Wifey.

"How the hell does she know where we live? Wes swore she didn't know and now the bitch is sending shit to my home threatening to harm my baby," I cried as tears rolled down my face.

"This is getting out of hand. I'm about to call Wes, because he needs to find this woman. Don't throw anything away. Everything you receive from her is evidence. Build a case like the police said," Beverly said as she got up to get her cellphone.

I was scared but that's not the reason I was crying. The tears were because I couldn't reach out and touch Shanell and snap her muthafuckin' neck.

Chapter 15
Shanell

I knew Justice was going to ignore my message and I had something else up my sleeve to get her attention. It was wrong for me to get a doll custom made to look like Faith. I took a picture of her the night I bonded with her at the hospital. I fell in love with the little girl and wished she was mine. If it wasn't for the band on her ankle, I would've taken her with me that night and disappeared. I would've been caught the minute I tried to take her off the floor of the hospital.

Wifey should've been having a nervous breakdown after seeing the gift I had delivered to her home and I would've loved to be the fly on the wall to see her reaction. That vision had to wait because I had other devious shit to attend to. I was driving toward Citywide Architects to pay the love of my life a visit.

Wes was very predictable and I knew exactly when he went out for lunch. Parking across from his job at exactly one o'clock, I saw him exit the building and walked up the street toward Chipotle. We had met at that exact spot on many occasions throughout the years. Now he didn't even bother checking on me, and it infuriated me to the core. I waited until he was out of sight before I got out of my car and ran across the street to the parking garage.

Jogging to section C, I looked for his black Benz and it wasn't in its usual spot. Knowing he was trying to throw me for a loop, I checked a couple rows back and bingo, there it was. I reached into the pocket of my jacket and removed the knife I brought for this occasion.

Walking around Wes's car a couple of times, I punctured his back tire and pulled down on the handle. The car slumped to the side and I laughed out loud and moved to the front tire and repeated the action. Once all four tires were flat, I still wasn't satisfied. Running the knife back and forth along his paint job, I fucked up his paint job and it was going to cost a pretty penny to get repaired.

I had spent enough time in the garage and headed for the stairwell but a pipe that was propped against the wall caught my attention. Without thinking I picked it up and went back to Wes's car and busted out all of his windows. I even broke his headlights and the taillights. At that point, I was satisfied with a job well done.

Creeping out of the garage, I glanced down the street and made a dash for my car. I merged into traffic just as Wes appeared in my rearview mirror. He was going to learn not to fuck with a woman scorned, because the end results weren't going to be anything he wanted in his life. Laughing all the way home, I listened to Jazmine Sullivan's *"Bust Your Windows"*.

When I made it to the south side, I stopped at Harold's Chicken Shack and got me a six-piece wing with lots of mild sauce and a large order of gizzards. The commute to my house was a breeze because everyone was still at work. Unlocking the door to my apartment, I stepped inside, locked the door, and dropped my keys on the island as I walked to my bedroom. I picked up the remote and went right to the ID channel to watch the crazy bitches kill their husbands.

Getting comfortable on my queen-sized bed, I opened my food and took a bite out of a piece of chicken. I tuned into the show that was on and this woman tried to hire a man to kill her husband and he was an undercover cop. Her best friend snitched on her ass and now she was in the interrogation room trying to plead her case. That was the reason I didn't tell anyone what my plans for Wes and his wife were.

Bria didn't even know because she was still his sister and I only trusted her as far as I could see. I had enough secrets to make her go into hiding for the rest of her life, so she knew not to fuck with me on that level. I was pissed at her because she told me what hospital Justice was in, but she wouldn't tell me where they lived. Bria told me where the bitch worked, who her best friend was, and she also told me where the best friend lived and worked. Maybe I should harass her ass too.

Wes led me to his home a couple weeks ago when I followed him home from work. He usually was good about watching his surroundings but he wasn't on his shit that day. I made sure to stay a great distance away but when he pulled into the driveway, I wanted to throw a cocktail bomb through the window.

Wes had me living in an apartment on the other side of the city while he and his wife lived in a big-ass house in the suburbs. I couldn't hold it in a minute longer without letting them know I still had eyes on them. Hopefully, Justice got tired of me making their lives a living hell and left. Then maybe I could get my man back and live happily ever after.

I finished my food and got up and went to throw the trash in the garbage. There was a knock on my door and I knew exactly who was on the other side. I wouldn't dare tell too many people where I lay my head. I'd been doing the most as of late. I peeked through the peephole and Curt was looking around nervously as he waited for me to open the door.

"Hey," I said through the partially-opened door.

"Damn, you gon' let me in or what?"

Moving to the side, I allowed Curt to enter, but I really didn't want to deal with him. Slowly locking the door, I turned to see him with his feet on my damn glass table with the remote in his hand. Politely walking over, I knocked his shit down and sat beside him on the couch.

"What brings you here without calling?" I asked.

"Shit, I help pay the bills. I don't have to call you to come over. Plus, I want my dick sucked."

Who the fuck did he think he was, Wes? That's the only person that could get that type of treatment out of me. "You got me confused with yo' bitch. We ain't the same, nigga."

Curt had been giving me money to pay my bills, but it was nothing compared to how I was living with Wes. The apartment I lived in had roaches and I found myself cleaning and bleaching every time I saw one of them nasty-ass things. It wasn't bad as when I first moved in because I had bombed the place three times in the last couple months. A few more times and I might be good.

"Why do you always have to bring my girl up when you talking to me? When I'm here with you, that's all you should be worried about, Shanell. Damn, a nigga can't get no lovin'?"

"Shouldn't you be at work?" I asked, ignoring all the other shit he said.

"I'm doing deliveries today so I'm trying to kill two birds with one stone. What's it gonna be? I don't have all day."

"You better be lucky I need you to knock the cobwebs out my pussy. Just to be clear, you don't have all day, right?" I asked, rolling my eyes.

"Yeah, I have fifteen minutes or less, actually."

"I guess that means you won't be getting yo' dick sucked," I smirked. "Ain't shit mediocre about me," I said, standing to my feet and pulling my pants down my hips.

Curt jumped to his feet and let his pants fall to the floor. He bent me over the arm of the couch and tried to force his joint into my love box. She wasn't responding because she was drier than the Sahara Desert. When his ass tried to spit start my shit, I almost cussed him out, but I just wanted him to start and finish at the same damn time. I helped him out by thinking of an encounter between Wes and me to get my juices flowing.

"Oh shit! I knew I could come get this wet shit," he moaned in my ear soon as he was able to slide in and out of my tunnel.

My eyes were shut tight, envisioning Wes caressing my folds and touching my ovaries. I was at my peak as I squeezed my muscles to make him cum when I wanted him to. Throwing my ass into his pelvis, his grip got tighter and his nails dug into my skin.

"Fuck, I'm cummin'!" I screamed out in pleasure.

"Me too! Let that shit out," Curt grunted from behind me as he let his babies coat my canal. I milked his ass for all he was worth, knowing I had stopped taking my birth control months prior and I needed to get pregnant.

His meat became flaccid and slipped out of my kitty with ease. Curt wasted no time going into the bathroom to clean himself up. I laid back on the couch and put my legs in the air.

When Curt walked back into the living room, he stood looking at me puzzled. "What are you doing?" he asked.

"I'm trying to stretch these cramps out of my legs," I faked cried, holding the back of my legs. Curt started massaging both of my calves and I closed my eyes to so he wouldn't see the deception within them. "Okay, that's better," I said, lowering my legs.

"I gotta get out of here. I have something for you," he said, going in his pocket for what I knew was money. "Buy yourself something nice and I'll see you in a couple days."

Frowning at the two crisp one hundred-dollar bills, I glanced up at him, unimpressed. "What am I supposed to do with that? There's nothing nice for me to buy with two hundred dollars, Curt. My rent is about to be due."

"That's all I got on me, Shanell. I'll Cash App the rent money to you. For now, I have to get back to work," he said, leaning down and kissing me on the cheek.

I didn't bother getting up to walk him to the door. Once he was gone, I got up and locked the door and went to take a shower. Curt had no idea he was nothing but a ploy in my game of deceit. Hopefully I'd created a baby out of the ordeal.

Chapter 16
Wes

I was in a meeting and had left my phone in my office, so I didn't get the call from my mother until lunchtime. When I got back to work after getting a steak and chicken burrito bowl from Chipotle, I got settled behind my desk and returned the call to my mother. As soon as she answered, I knew something was wrong.

"Weston King Junior, how the hell did Shanell find out where you live?" Were the first words she said to me. I didn't know how to reply because I had no clue the bitch knew my address.

"Ma, Shanell doesn't know. I never let her know I purchased a home for me and Justice. Where is this coming from?" I asked, shoving a spoonful of food in my mouth.

"There isn't anyone else dumb enough to send a lookalike doll of Faith with a bloody knife sticking out the chest but her. This shit is going too far, son. Shanell is going to hurt somebody. She also sent Justice another message on that damn Spacebook shit."

I couldn't believe what I was hearing. Shanell had been quiet for the most part and I thought she had come to her senses that we were over. I ran my hand over my face because I didn't know where to start looking for Shanell. Hell, I didn't know if she even had a place to live since I forced her out of the apartment.

"Ma, is Justice alright?" I asked, concerned. "Do I need to come home?"

"She's fine and no, I'm going to stay here until you get home. There's no telling what Shanell is about to be up to. If she shows up at this house, she will die. I'm not going to play these childish games with somebody else's child. Shit, I didn't play that bullshit with my own. I wanted you to know what's going on so you can get to the bottom of it."

"I'll make a couple calls and try to figure things out. I'll be home fast as traffic allows. I love you, Ma. Tell Justice don't worry. I got this." Ending the call, I thought about who I could call to get information on Shanell and my stupid-ass sister came to mind.

Eating half of my lunch, I picked up my phone and dialed Bria's number. She sent me to voicemail and I dialed her ass right back.

"What is it, Wes? I'm in the middle of something right now."

"Hello to you too, little sister. This won't take long at all. Have you heard from Shanell?" I asked in between bites.

"Why are you concerned about Nell, Wes? I'm quite sure she's living her best life since you made her a homeless person."

"Living her best life is far from the truth. I need to know where she is and you will tell me, Bria."

"I'm not telling you shit! Why would I betray my friend because you don't want to leave well enough alone? Worry about your wife and child, bro. Leave Shanell alone."

"I'm not bothering Shanell! The bitch cost me plenty of money for wrecking the apartment, she tried to kidnap my daughter from the hospital, she's been harassing my wife, and now she wants to send bloody dolls to my house! Speaking of that, I hope you didn't tell her where I live, Bria."

"Hell nawl! I already told you I wouldn't do that. I knew about her destroying the apartment and I also knew about her showing up at the hospital. I didn't know anything about all the other shit she has done. Wes, I will talk to her, but I will not give you her number."

"If anyone gets hurt behind her foolishness, yo' ass will be partially to blame. How the fuck you not going to ride with your family on this, Bria? I'm not going to do anything to her. All I want to tell her is stay the fuck away from me and mine!"

"Wes, I don't have shit to do with any—"

"You're protecting the bitch even though she's wrong! You have everything to do with it because I don't believe you didn't know," I said, cutting her off.

"Are we going to McDonald's?" I heard a child say in the background.

"Whose kid do you have?" I questioned.

"That's my neighbor's son. I'm babysitting. I have to go," Bria said in a rush, ending the call.

I didn't know what the hell my sister had going on, but her secrets were going to come out sooner than later. After finishing my lunch, I completed paperwork that needed to be submitted and then I started on a new drawing of a building a well-known businessman wanted drawn up. By the time I was done, I realized it was four o'clock. After straightening my desk, I grabbed my briefcase and headed out of the office. I said my goodbyes and made my way to the garage so I could get home to my family.

The thought of seeing Faith had me rushing to the elevator. As I stepped into the garage, an eerie feeling came over me as I walked in the direction I parked. Knowing Shanell knew where I worked and the fact she knew where I parked my car, I had parked in a different section of the garage. Hitting the button on my key fob, the lights blinked and the horn sounded, letting me know exactly where I parked my ride.

The closer I got to my car, the faster I walked. The window appeared to be down on the driver's side and I knew it wasn't that way when I got out of it. Once the car was in view, my heart stopped. My shit was fucked up! All my windows were busted, the paint job was destroyed, and all four tires weren't even repairable.

Shanell was the first person I thought of when I saw the damage done to my ride. The call from my mother rang in my ears and I was ready to kill the bitch. Calling the police immediately, I paced back forth as I waited for them to arrive. Holding my head high, I asked God for forgiveness beforehand because when I caught up with Shanell, she was going straight to the hospital. She was taking shit too far and need to face the fact that we were over.

I contacted the insurance company after taking pictures, then I decided to call Dap for a ride.

"Bro, what's up?" he asked without saying hello.

"I need you to come to my job. My car won't start and I need a ride to the crib." Already knowing how he would react, I opted not to tell him the truth. I'd rather have peace of mind until he actually saw the damage for himself.

"You're lucky I'm at Customs with the contractors. Give me a minute and I'll be there,"

"Okay, thanks, man, I appreciate it."

"No problem," he said hanging up.

My blood boiled every time I looked at my fuckin' car. Staring straight ahead, I noticed a camera at the far end of the garage. It prompted me to survey the area where my car was parked. Dialing the number for the security desk in the building, I waited anxiously for someone to answer.

"Citywide Security, how may I help you?"

"Yes, this is Weston King from the fifteenth floor. My car was vandalized in the garage and I was wondering if you could pull the video for Section C."

"Damn, man, you're shitting me, right? This is Earl, I'm on that shit right now, big homie. I'll hit yo' line back soon as I find something."

"Okay, thanks. The police just pulled in, I gotta go."

The patrol car pulled behind my car after I waved them over. Two officers exited the vehicle and started processing the damage. One of the officers shook his head as his partner walked slowly to the other side.

"Who did you piss off? They did a number on your vehicle. This looks like a job of a very angry woman. Any idea who may have done this?" The officer stated as he turned to face me. The name on his nametag read Carter.

"Officer Carter, I know for a fact it was a woman that destroyed my car. Her name is Shanell Jones and I've been having problems with her since I broke things off with her. She has also been harassing my wife," I explained.

"What proof do you have that Miss Jones did all the things you claim?" Officer Carter asked.

"I have text and social media messages of her admitting everything she has done. Her real name isn't connected to anything, but I know it's her."

Officer Carter tilted his head to the side as if he didn't believe what I was saying. Like the officers from the hospital, I had a feeling nothing would be done about this situation either.

"Without concrete evidence, we don't have a case, sir. The most I can do is write up a police report for you to show your insurance company. You do have insurance, don't you?"

"Yeah," I responded as my phone rang. Glancing down at the screen, I saw that it was Earl calling back. "Please tell me you have something," I said when I answered.

"The vandalism was definitely caught on video. It's hard to see who it was, but bring them up to take a look."

"I'm on my way, Earl. Thanks." I turned to the officers and took a deep breath. "Security just informed me the incident was caught on video. The proof you said I needed is upstairs. Would you mind coming to view it with me?"

"That's exactly what we need. Lead the way," Officer Carter said.

We all entered the elevator and went to the first floor. I led the way to the security desk where Earl and his supervisor Jerome stood studying one of the surveillance monitors. Earl glanced up, motioning us over as he pointed at the screen.

"Good evening, fellas. I'm Officer Carter and this is my partner, Officer Reynolds. What do you have for us?"

"We've watched the footage numerous times, but unfortunately, the video is grainy and there's no way to determine who actually vandalized Mr. King's property. The body structure is indeed of a woman but her face isn't visible no matter how much we zoomed in on the image," Jerome said.

"That's Shanell! I know for a fact that's her!" I exclaimed, pointing at the monitor.

"Mr. King, her face is not visible so there's not enough proof it's her," Officer Reynolds shot back.

"I bought that damn hat for her! What more has to happen before y'all take me serious about this bitch?" I was beyond pissed because the police were not doing their job.

"Mr. King, I'll write up a report for you but that's about all we can do. I'm sorry your car was damaged, but that's all we have until we can identify the person in the footage."

"Whatever. How long will that take? Because I want to get home to my family," I asked.

"No longer than ten minutes. Let's go back to the garage and I'll have the report written up quick as possible."

My phone rang again and it was Dap. "Bro, come to the garage, I'm on my way down there now. I have to get this report from the police."

"The police? What the fuck is going on, Wes?" Dap's voice boomed in my ear.

"I'll explain everything when you get to the garage. I'm getting on the elevator and the phone is going to cut off."

"Yeah, a'ight."

When we got to the garage, Dap was pulling in as I stepped off the elevator and he whipped into a vacant park spot and jumped out. "Wes, talk to me. What the hell is going on?" he asked, looking at the police officers.

"Mr. King, I'll get started on the report so you can head out," Officer Carter said as he headed to his cruiser.

All of this shit was starting to take a toll on me and I just wanted it to end, but Shanell wasn't going to stop until I suffered to the point of no return.

Meesha

Chapter 17
Dap

Wes had yet to answer my question, but when the officer said he would have the report ready soon, it confused the shit out of me. Wes said he needed a ride because his car wouldn't start. I saw that was a damn lie for sure. He stood back with a goofy-ass expression on his face, and it only pissed me off.

"Since when do the police write up a report for a vehicle that won't start?" I asked Wes as the officers walked away. Instead of him answering, he too walked away through parked cars. "Do you hear me talking to you, brah?" He stopped in front of his car and I couldn't believe the damage that was done to his whip.

Wes opened his mouth and I held my hand up to stop him from speaking. "Why didn't you just tell me what the fuck was going on when you called me?"

"I didn't say anything because I didn't want to get interrogated by you thirty minutes ago. The way my anger had heightened, I would've unleashed my anger on you. I have enough shit to deal with right now."

"Shanell did this shit?" I asked, folding my arms over my chest.

"According to the video, there's a woman seen tearing my shit up with a pipe. The image wasn't clear and the police is still talking about there's no evidence."

"So, she's going to get away once again, huh?"

"It seems that way because her face wasn't visible on the video. It had to be her. Who else is mad at me? No mutha-fuckin' body. Plus, she found out where I lived somehow. Mama called and said she sent a doll to the house and it had a bloody knife sticking out the chest. That's not the worst part though. The damn doll looked like Faith."

"What type of shit is this bitch on, brah? When did that take place?" I asked.

"I got the call at about one o'clock—"

"One o'clock? Nigga, why the fuck you didn't call me then? It's almost five o'clock and you still downtown diggin' in yo' ass. This shit could've waited until you checked on your family!"

"My mama said she had it and I didn't need to rush to the house." If looks could kill, his ass would've had two slugs in both eyes.

"Fuck all that! You don't need nobody to tell you what to do, Wes! Where is that grown-ass man you were talking about not too long ago? Shanell got yo' ass shaking in your penny loafers looking like a chump, nigga. Bring the nigga from the streets back because this corporate nigga ain't cuttin' it!"

I wanted to punch him in his shit because he wasn't thinking about the severity of the situation.

The officers walked over and the shorter officer had his hand on his gun like I was a fuckin' criminal or something. The taller one had a piece of paper in his hand as he walked up to us.

"Mr. King, is everything okay?" the taller officer asked.

"Hell nawl, he's not okay! Are y'all going to arrest Shanell Jones for this shit?" I asked roughly.

"And you are?" the shorter officer asked.

"Who the fuck is you? Don't ask a question with a question. Answer my question and I'll think about answering yours."

"I'm Officer Carter and this is my partner, Officer Reynolds. To answer you other question, we can't apprehend anyone without proof the person committed a crime. We will do all we can to try to identify the person in the video, but it's going to be hard due to the fact the video isn't high quality. Now, who are you again?" Officer Carter asked.

"I'm his brother. But you're worried about the wrong shit. Shanell is the one that did this and many other things as well in the past couple months. When will the Chicago Police start doing the job y'all are paid to do? All I want to know is when are y'all going to lock her crazy ass up before she hurts somebody?"

"There's not enough evidence—"

"Bullshit! Wes, let's go, now! Y'all ain't saying shit I want to hear and nothing will be done once again." I walked away to my car and stood waiting on Wes.

The officer gave Wes the report and said something to him that I couldn't hear, but the way he eyeballed me I knew he was talking about me in some type of manner. Wes was responding and shaking his head, obviously not getting anything new out of the pigs. Everything that has happened is all on him because he should've left the bitch alone like he did when he was locked up. Wes would've avoided a shit load of drama had he listened.

There was no way a bitch would be able to get that close to my family and have me obtaining a muthafuckin' police report. Fuck the police! His ass should be tracking Shanell down and whooping her ass! Wes opened the passenger door and I was ready to tear into his ass as soon as he sat the fuck down in the seat.

"Brah, don't call the pigs for shit else! They didn't do shit when Shanell pulled that stunt at the hospital and they're definitely not going to do shit about this either. Where can she be?"

"I don't know! I called Bria to find out what she knows, but she refused to give up any information. Not even Shanell's phone number."

"Bria's muthafuckin' ass is loyal to someone that don't have our blood running through their damn veins. She has been covering up Shanell's dirt for years, but this time it's serious and she still on the wrong side of the fence. I've never seen a sister go against her brother the way she has. Sister or not, you better watch her ass too."

I started the car and pulled out of the garage to get my brother's stupid ass home. I hit the expressway and Wes sat in the passenger seat making call after call while my mind was on ways to kill Shanell if I came in contact with her. When Wes told me about what she did to my niece, I almost punched him in his shit every time he said "let the police handle it" and look at them, not handling a damn thing.

Ten minutes into the ride, Wes had arranged for a tow truck to take his car to the auto body shop and returned a call to the insurance company. It seemed like he was more worried about that damn car than his fuckin' wife. Shanell was just getting started and he needed to get his mind right so he would be ready for whatever she came with next time.

"What's your problem with Bria, bro? Sometimes you don't even act like she's your sister," Wes said, cutting into my thoughts.

"Bria is my sister only because she is a product of my daddy's nut sack. I don't fuck with her because she is shady as hell and I won't act like I don't see the bullshit she be on like the rest of y'all. She's sneaky and don't value family. We all have done for her spoiled ass but she always gives us her ass to kiss. You should be asking her why she's constantly stabbing you in the back and twisting that muthafucka."

"You know Bria and Shanell have been friends since the day I brought her around. I won't hold her responsible for what Shanell decided to do."

"You sound dumb as fuck, Wes. Bria has known Shanell for nine years and has been your brother all her fuckin' life! Nothing comes between family, my nigga. I don't care what kind of fallout occurs; your sibling is always going to have your back. Especially if the bitch she calls her friend is trying to harm your family."

Wes sat in the passenger seat looking stupid, which wasn't anything new as of late. He wasn't comprehending anything that was told to him, and I wanted to beat his ass for being so fuckin' soft. All he wanted to do was give the benefit of the doubt to everybody instead of going to war to protect his fuckin' family.

"Something is going on with Bria and she's not saying what it is. What I do know is, she's blaming us for whatever it is. That's not including Daddy though. Before you ask any questions, I'll give you an example. When Bria comes home, who do she gravitate to?"

Wes was quiet for a minute before answering. "She spends most of her time with Pops or she's in the streets."

"Exactly. How often do she interact with Mama Beverly without cussing and having an attitude? She doesn't. When you were locked up, any mention of your name and she would storm off. What sets her off is something I don't know, but I have a feeling we will learn the reasons behind her jealousy."

"Dap, Bria has nothing to be jealous about. Trust me, you got shit all wrong," Wes said as I parked on the street in front of his house.

I couldn't park in the driveway because there were several cars taking up the available space and my father's car was one of them. Wes hurried out of the car and up the steps to the front door. It was too late for him to move swiftly, in my opinion. He should've moved like lightning when he heard what happened at his house earlier. I took my time going inside because my brother was about to get his ass handed to him on a platter.

"If this bitch does one more thing to this family, I'm whooping your ass!" was what I heard as I made my way inside the door. "I've played Mrs. Nice Guy too long and I'm done with this shit, Wes. This is your doing! All you had to do was tell her crazy ass the truth instead of trying to be sneaky!"

Justice was in Wes's face like she wanted to smack fire from him. Pops stood between the two of them because the way the scene was set up, it looked as if Justice had to be pulled off Wes. The anger was evident on her face and I wouldn't have wanted to be in my brother's shoes.

The look on Pops' face was one that seemed as if he was reliving the shit he had gone through back in the day. Justice was standing firm in a pair of jean pants with a Pink black and white T-shirt and a pair of socks. Her hair was in a messy bun and her face was clear of makeup, but it was scrunched up in a scowl that meant she was not taking any more shit from anybody.

"Justice, I understand your frustration."

"Do you, Wes? The bitch sent a damn doll that looked like our daughter to this house with a knife sticking out of it. That was hours ago!" Justice screamed, leaning around my father then holding her hands up. She shook her head as she backed up a little bit before turning to go into the kitchen.

I took that moment to glance around the room. Tana, Justice's best friend, was holding Faith as she fed her and Beverly was sitting on the arm of the sofa with her eyes trained on Wes. My attention went back to Tana because her beauty was captivating to me.

From her almond-shaped eyes, I envisioned her luscious lips against mine while grabbing her natural curly hair tightly in my hand. The last time I saw Tana was when we were at the hospital. If it wasn't for Shanell's messy ass barging in, I would've gotten the chance to get to know her. Nothing was going to stop me from shooting my shot after things died down with Wes.

Beverly's voice took me out of my trance and once I focused, Tana was staring at me with a smirk on her face.

"In his defense, Justice, I told Wes it wasn't necessary for him to come home. That's why I called my husband to come over here," Beverly explained.

Marching back into the room with a glass of water in hand, Justice stood in front of Beverly. "No disrespect, Mama Beverly, but Faith and I are Wes's responsibility. He should've made like Superman and got here regardless of what you told him." Justice wasn't trying to hear shit anybody was saying and I didn't blame her. There was nothing wrong about how she felt.

"I wouldn't have been able to get here quickly because my car was vandalized in the garage of my job," Wes said, looking defeated.

"Oh, the bitch made her rounds today, I see," Justice said sarcastically as she sipped from the glass she was holding.

"What did she do to your car?" Beverly barked.

"Shanell fucked that Benz up! Let's just say, he'll be flossin' in the Lexus from here on out." I laughed. "My bad for laughing, bro, but I told you so."

Wes cut his eyes at me and I didn't care because I did tell his ass to leave that hoe alone. He had to deal with the consequences however they came at him. I hated that Justice and Faith were caught in the middle though. My father gave me the "cut it out" look he always used to when we were younger. I was no longer that little boy so the shit wasn't going to work on me. Wes maybe, but not Dap.

"Shanell messed up my paint job, busted all the windows, and destroyed all four tires. I had to contact the insurance company and the police so I would have a report on hand," Wes said, breaking down the damage done on his car.

Justice took a seat on the loveseat as Wes's eyes followed her every move. "Let me guess: the police still didn't do anything, huh?"

"You got that right. They didn't do shit even though Wes identified Shanell's raggedy ass on the video."

"Donovan!" my father yelled. "Your brother is going through enough as is."

"And why is he going through all of this, Pop? Keep that in mind," I shot back. "Hold his ass accountable for his fuck ups is all I'm saying."

Wes stalked over and pushed me in the chest, "Why are you against me all of a sudden? I thought you had my back, brah! What happened to that?"

"I will always have your back! What I won't do is let you stand here like all of this is just going to go away. It's not! I'm not going to sugarcoat shit for you, but what I will do is tell you what you don't want to hear. You fucked up when you didn't leave Shanell where she was when you got out of prison," I barked, standing firm on what the fuck I was saying. Pops walked over as a precaution, I guess, but I swear if my brother took a shot at me, it was going to be on.

"You have a good woman and you continued to deal with a bitch that was fuckin' with the homie. Wes, you have to deal with this shit head on. Allowing Shanell to continue plotting on you is the wrong move to make. You have to put in the work to find her." Babying Wes was the last thing I was going to do. I'd leave that shit to my father and Beverly.

"Okay, wait a minute, both of you calm the fuck down. Arguing and fighting is not going to make this shit just disappear. The two of you have been tighter than tight all your lives, and this shit with Shanell is not going to break that bond. Not now, not ever!"

My father was mad as fuck, but I meant everything I said to Wes. He needed to hear the truth, and I gave him the raw version. Sitting in the chair next to where we stood, I wiped my hands on my pants leg and sat back without intending to say another word.

"Son, do you know where Shanell is now?" my father asked.

"No. I called Bria, but she refused to tell me where she lived and she wouldn't even give me her phone number. Pop, you should give her a call to see if she would tell you what she refuses to tell me."

"I'll give her a call, because this shit is getting out of hand," my father said, running his hand down his face. "This is worse than the shit I had to go through. These New Age women are deadly and don't know how to accept rejection."

"Wes Senior, this is not all of Shanell's fault. The way you said that makes it seem as if Wes had no part in what has taken place. I don't agree with the way she is handling the situation, but when a woman's scorned, you don't know what she will do after the fact," Tana said. "I'm standing ten toes down with Justice and the bitch will die fucking with two females from the street."

"Baby girl, at no point did I say my son was innocent in any of this. He played a major part, but what Shanell has done is on her. Wes, Justice," he said, turning his body so he could see the two of them, "I'm here for you guys one hundred percent. Don't stress yourselves over this because we will get through this together."

"It's too late. I'm stressed to the max because once again, this woman has gotten close to my family," Justice said, standing to her feet. "Wes, I've booked a ticket to spend a couple days with my parents just to breathe normally for a change. Faith and I are leaving in the morning. Hopefully when I return Sunday, all of this drama will be a thing of the past."

"Baby—"

"Wes, I won't let you try to talk me out of going and I'm not asking for your permission. I miss my parents and I'm tired of the bullshit going on here. I need some time away from all of this. You are more than welcome to join us, but with or without you, me and my baby will be on that plane."

"I have an important meeting on Friday. I can't leave, Justice! You should wait until we can go together, babe."

"Did we start this bullshit together? Case closed. Handle your business and I'll handle mine. I need to leave before I do something I regret. Faith needs me in this world and your crazy ex is going to make me end up putting hands and feet on her ass. Thank y'all for coming to check on me," Justice said, addressing everyone in the room.

"I'm going to lie down before I start packing for my trip." She turned to Tana, "Sis, can you get her at six so I can get to the airport on time?"

"I think it would be better if I stayed the night. I took the rest of the week off before I left school for the day. I'm on the same flight as you. I know you didn't think I was going to let you go alone, did you?" Tana responded with a smile.

"Nah, I knew you would make arrangements with your slick ass," Justice said, bending over to take Faith from Tana's arms.

Instead of handing Faith over, Tana moved her out of Justice's reach. "I got her. Go rest up and I'll be here if you need me."

Justice waved her hand in the air and headed up the stairs. Wes started to follow her, but my father stopped him by holding his hand to his chest.

"Give her a little time, son. The last thing you want to do is try to force her into not going. Use this time wisely, Wes. Your mother and I are about to head out. Don't hesitate to call."

Beverly pulled her jacket over her arms and hugged Wes tightly. I stood to my feet and hugged her goodbye as well. Wes walked with them to the door and watched until they pulled out of the driveway. After looking around a couple times, he shut the door and locked it.

"Brah, you got some green on you?"

I looked at him like he was crazy because Wes hadn't smoked since he got the job at Citywide. Weed was probably what he needed to get him in the right frame of mind to deal with Shanell. Instead of responding, I went out to my ride to get the ultimate package out of the trunk. Hell, I wanted to blaze up myself anyway.

Meesha

Chapter 18
Tana

The things that were going on with this Shanell person was some shit right out of a movie. Who hides a baby in a hospital, sends a bloody doll to someone's house, and destroys property? All because a man doesn't want them anymore. When the relationship is over, walk the fuck away and boss up on the nigga.

As soon as Wes and Dap went out to the backyard, my phone rang. I looked down and saw Miss Beverly's name on display. Already knowing what she was going to say, I answered the promptly.

"Hello."

"Montana, when were you going to tell me you were leaving with Justice? We have plans," Beverly said into my ear.

"I know, and we will be back Sunday afternoon, I promise. Don't worry, I'll have her at the venue on time."

"Take care of her, Tana. Justice is going through so much. This is supposed to be a happy time for her and Shanell is making it miserable."

"To be honest with you, Beverly, Justice is far from miserable. I can speak on how she's feeling because we're cut from the same cloth. She's trying to get away from the situation for a minute before she hurts somebody." I chuckled.

"If Shanell keeps coming for her family, her body is going to be found at the bottom of Lake Michigan with cement blocks attached to her ankles. The way we grew up, is not how either one of us lives today. We both have changed for the better, but it will take shit like this to convert us back. Excuse my language," I said, looking down at a sleeping Faith.

"I understand all of what you're saying and I get it. Shanell is going to get her ass beat and I would turn a blind eye whenever it happens. Enjoy your trip and I will let you go."

"Goodnight, Beverly. Thanks for being there to help Justice. Talk to you later," I said, ending the call.

I stood from the sofa and climbed the stairs to put Faith to bed. After covering her with the light blanket, I turned the baby monitor on and softly closed the door before making my way to Justice's bedroom. She was packing clothes into her luggage with a scowl on her face.

"You good, sis?" I asked, sitting on the end of the bed.

"I will be." She smiled. "This bitch is really pushing major buttons and I feel myself going back to our high school days. Not the immature time, but the 'I don't give a fuck I will beat your ass' time. You of all people knows how much I hated the person I was back then."

"Both of us were standing side by side every time something went down. If we were caught alone, we went back together and settled that shit. Ain't nothing changed. However, we will go to Arizona and let Wes deal with his mistake."

"Tana, you can stop calling this a mistake. A mistake would be one time. My husband just stopped fuckin' with this woman a couple months ago. That's not a muthafuckin' mistake! He knew what he was doing and there's no telling how long it would've continued if he wasn't forced to tell me about it."

Justice was right about what she said and I agreed. My friend was a good one because I didn't think I would've been able to stay with my husband if the shoe was on the other foot. Justice was strong and was willing to stick it out. My eyes went to the door and Wes was standing in the doorway. That was my cue to get up to leave so they could talk in private.

Closing the door behind me, I walked down the stairs and went straight to the kitchen to cook something for dinner. With everything going on, Justice didn't think about trying to cook. As I opened the refrigerator, I heard movement behind me and turned around. Dap was standing by the island and he was fine as hell.

"What you doing?" he asked, stepping into the kitchen.

"I'm hungry as hell so I figured I'd cook something for us to eat."

"Nah, let's go out and get some wings or something. It's going to take too long to cook and it's getting late," he suggested. "What do you say?"

I was hungry and this man was giving me a solution to my problem. I didn't know him, but he was Wes's brother and I was sure he wouldn't do anything to hurt me. Letting my eyes travel from the top of his head to his shoes, I loved what I saw. Dap had on a simple white T-shirt that had Customs by Dap printed on the front, black jeans, and a pair of black and white Jordans on his feet.

"Yeah, why not? I'm down, but I don't want chicken. We can bring that back for Justice and Wes. I want some fish."

"That's cool. I'll place an order then we can go pick the food up and come back," he said, pulling out his phone.

I grabbed a bottled water and leaned against the counter as I twisted the top off. Dap ordered the food and took a seat at the table. Figuring I'd use the time we waited to get more information on Shanell's trifling ass, I sat across from him and cleared my throat.

"What's the back story on this bitch, Dap? Who the fuck is she?" I asked, taking a sip of the water.

"Shanell has been around for years and Wes saved her when he met her downtown. She didn't know anyone in Chicago and didn't have any money. Wes put her up in a hotel and eventually moved her into his apartment. Shanell grew on Wes because she wasn't the type of female he usually entertained. I believe he actually felt sorry for her."

Listening to Dap run the story by me, I kind of felt sorry for how Shanell had to make do back in the day.

"He was never in love with her, but had mad love for her because she was loyal and helped him make a lot of money in the streets. They appeared to be a couple and when Shanell became pregnant, Wes stepped up to take care of his responsibility. Six months later, Wes was arrested and sentenced to four years in jail."

"And that's when she cheated with his friend," I said, throwing what I knew out at him.

"Yep. Shanell left my brother to fend for himself while he was locked up. She was too busy parading around with Curt. Hell yeah, I told my brother about that shit because he had a right to know."

"If you hadn't told him about her infidelities you would've been an ain't-shit-ass brother in my eyes. So, you did the right thing in that aspect. Why do you think Wes didn't stop messing around with her when he got with Justice?" I asked, digging deep.

"I'll tell you why when we get in the car," he said, getting up from the chair.

I followed suit and walked out the kitchen behind him. Dap had a pair of bowed legs that told me he had a thick piece of wood in his pants. I'd dated a few guys in my lifetime, and that myth hadn't failed me yet. As I slipped my waist-length leather jacket on, I sent Justice a text letting her know where I was going.

Jus: Don't slip on his dick. I've peeped how he looks at you.

I didn't bother responding to her because wasn't nothing happening between me and Dap. We were going to pick up food and that was it. Other than learning about Shanell, there was nothing else we had to talk about.

Dap led the way to his car, which was parked on the street. He automatically opened the door like a gentleman and I wasted no time taking advantage of his kind gesture.

Dap got into the driver seat and I looked at the clock on the dash to prevent myself from looking at him. He started the car and left it running for a minute before pulling off. We cruised for about five minutes before he started answering the question I'd asked back at the house.

"To answer your question about why Wes didn't leave Shanell alone, I can't answer that because I don't know his reasons. But I can give you my take on it. When Shanell lost the baby, Wes was fucked up behind it. Shanell, on the other hand, was put on suicide watch and prescribed medication.

"Shanell manipulated the shit outta that man but he never saw what she was doing. He would get mad when I tried to open his eyes so he could see the shit she was spitting was bullshit. I left a month after he got out and only talked about what they had going on when he brought it up. Wes told me about Justice, but failed to tell me he was still dealing with Shanell. I found out about them when all of this drama started."

Dap parked in front of Nick's and threw the gear in park. We got out and walked inside of the restaurant. He went up to the counter and I sat at an empty table and sat down. He came back and sat across from me. Talking about Wes and Shanell's situationship was something I no longer wanted to do. Dap must've felt the same way because he bypassed the subject.

"They said the food would be ready in about ten minutes. While we wait, tell me about Montana Taylor," he said, folding his hands on top of the table.

"What do you want to know?"

"What do you do for a living?"

"I'm an eighth grade school teacher at Culver Elementary. I've been teaching for the past five years."

"Being a teacher doesn't pay much. Do you like it?"

"It may sound crazy, but I don't teach for the money. There are a lot of kids that need more teachers that truly care about not only their education, but their wellbeing as well. I was twenty-two when I started teaching and I knew that wasn't my final stop. Being the principal is where I see myself in the future."

Dap was silent for a moment then he smiled. "You were twenty-two when you started teaching, you've been doing it for five years, so that would make you twenty-seven years old." He smirked.

"If you wanted to know my age, all you had to do was ask." I laughed. "Yes, I'm twenty-seven. How old are you, Dap?"

"First off, only the people in the streets and my brother calls me Dap. I would prefer if you called me Donovan."

"You are kind of Dapper, sir. I'll try to remember that from now on," I smiled. "Now, how old are you and what is it that you do for a living?"

"That's cute. I'm twenty-eight and I own my own business."

"I love to hear about our people starting businesses. Wait, what type of job is it? Please don't say you're a street pharmacist." I looked at Dap across the table and silently prayed that wasn't the case.

"Montana, never judge a book by its cover. My jewelry and the type of car I drive is probably why you came to that conclusion. I'll assure you, me being a drug dealer is far from the truth. I actually have a custom jewelry business called Customs by Dap. I started the business in my teens, but I was only selling T-shirts at the time.

"When I moved to California, I hooked up with this Italian dude name Rochus, but everybody called him Rocco. He taught me everything I needed to know about diamonds and jewels. Rocco was looking to retire, but didn't want to just close his business down so he handed it over to me."

"Someone that wasn't related to you just handed a whole business over to you? Why did he feel comfortable enough to do that?" I asked, amazed.

"I used to spend lots of money with Rocco when I first met him. Since we are being honest with one another, I used to sell drugs for many years. For years, Rocco helped me get my business off the ground as he slowly brought his clientele to Customs. I was still doing my thing on the street and I knew selling drugs was something I no longer wanted to do. I molded one of my young protégés to take over my drug business."

I looked down at my hands and there were plenty of questions running through my mind. Dap reached across the table and lifted my head up by my chin forcing me to look him in the face. "What's on your mind, Tana?"

"Why did you tell me all of this?" I asked.

"Tana, I want to get to know you and there's not a better way than to tell you about Donovan King and Dap the former Street King. I hope my story don't scare you away. There is more to my story and I would like to tell you if you're willing to listen."

"King, your order is ready," the young girl said from behind the counter.

Dap stood to get the food. He had ordered a large pan that could feed a party of ten.

My phone rang and Tyson was the person calling. Ignoring the call, I was about to put it back in my purse when it rang again. The ringing of my phone was aggravating me so I answered.

"What?" I barked.

"Why the fuck is you ignoring my calls, Tana?"

I laughed at his stupid ass. "Why are you calling me? I've told you countless times that we were over. You wanted to end things between us and I agreed. Now you want to act like I was the one that initiated all of this. Leave me alone and move the fuck on, Tyson."

"Everything okay, Tana? Is something wrong with Justice?" Dap asked, walking over to me.

"Who is that? I know you're not with another nigga, Tana."

"Don't worry about who I'm with. Worry about Rachel's ass. That's where you wanted to be, right? Goodbye, Tyson. Lose my damn number." Ending the call, I turned to Dap and nodded my head yes.

We left the restaurant and talked all the way back to the house and well into the morning.

Chapter 18
Wes

Justice was pissed and there was nothing I could say to make her feel any other way. When I went upstairs after smoking with Dap, that's where I stayed for the rest of the night. Tana brought us some fish, chicken, and fries to eat, but we did that in silence. Justice ended up going to sleep in the middle of me telling her how sorry I was. Faith soothed my soul when she started crying. I ended up falling asleep in her room as I watched her sleep after changing and feeding her.

The sun beamed in my eyes as I opened them. The elephants, giraffes, monkeys, lions, and all the other animals let me know I was still in the nursery. Turning my head to Faith's crib, I saw that it was empty.

I jumped to my feet. The rocking chair hit the wall as I rushed out of the room and down the hall to the bedroom I shared with Justice. The luggage she packed the night before was no longer sitting by the door. The bed was made and her purse, phone, and jacket were gone. There was a piece of paper lying on top of the comforter and I knew my wife and child were heading to Arizona.

I sat on the edge of the bed and picked up the paper. Glancing at the clock on my side of the bed, I saw the time was seven-thirty in the morning. I unfolded the paper and stared at Justice's neat penmanship.

Wes,

I didn't wake you before I left because I didn't want you to try talking me out of going to Arizona. It may seem as if I'm upset with you, but I'm not. I'm more disappointed because of the way you chose to handle your past. Remember, honesty is the best policy when it comes to me. I've forgiven you for the wrongs that you have done to our family, but I will never forget.

The hell Shanell is trying to put us through is a tactic to break us apart. We won't let that happen. When I get back, I want us to be happy again, Wes. We got married for a reason and we will live our happily ever after. It's going to be hard with a psycho basically stalking us, not knowing when she would strike again.

I want you to know that I love you with all my heart. This hiccup will not come between us. It's 'til death do us part, but the death part will be for you if you pull another stunt like this one.

Justice

I laughed nervously because there was much truth in Justice's words. I remembered her talking about the things of her past. I wasn't trying to see if she was about that life. I folded the paper and put it on the nightstand before reaching for my phone. Going to work was out of the question, so I decided to work from home instead.

After calling Stewart to let him know I wouldn't be in, I went downstairs to find something to eat. Entering the kitchen, I went straight for the refrigerator to see if there were any more chicken wings from the previous night. Surprisingly, there was still a big-ass pan filled with fish, chicken, and fries. Piling a plate filled with some of everything, I placed it in the microwave for two and a half minutes.

The alarm beeped, indicating someone had entered my home. I snatched the nine-millimeter that I kept in the kitchen drawer and walked slowly toward the living room. When I rounded the corner, Dap came face to face with my little friend.

"Whoa, nigga! What the fuck!" he exclaimed with his hands in the air.

"How the fuck you get in here?" I asked, lowering my tool, sticking it in the front of the shorts I wore.

"Justice gave me the spare key so I could get back in. I took them to the airport because I didn't think it was necessary for them to pay for leaving Tana's car there," he explained. "At least I know you still stay strapped. Why you not at work?" he asked, walking around me to enter the kitchen.

"I didn't feel like going. I'm working from home today." The microwave beeped and my breakfast was ready. Taking the plate out, I reached in the cabinet and grabbed the bottle of hot sauce. I got settled at the table and dug into my food. "You stayed here last night?"

"Yeah, it didn't make sense to go home. Tana and I stayed up talking most of the night and I actually enjoyed her company. It's been awhile since I've been in the presence of a woman and didn't fuck."

I watched my brother wash his hands at the sink with a big-ass Kool-Aid smile on his face, which was a first when it had something to do with a woman. The last time he smiled like that was when he Facetimed me after opening Customs by Dap. He hadn't talked about a love interest at all while he was in California. Hell, his life in California was pretty much a mystery to me.

"Tana is a very independent woman, brah. She can't be bought like the females you were fucking with before you left. If you are going to go after her, you're gonna have to come correct. She's the best friend to my wife, and you've witnessed the type of woman she is."

"Justice isn't playing with yo' ass at all. On the way to the airport, she told me to find Shanell and blow her muthafuckin' head off." Dap laughed as he fixed a plate for himself. "Man, bro, she is ready to fuck that girl all the way up. I hope Pop gets Shanell's number or something from Bria so somebody can talk her into leaving this shit alone."

With Dap mentioning my father, I got up and ran upstairs to get my phone. I had a missed call from Justice and I tried to call her back, but the phone went into voicemail. As I skipped down the steps, my phone rang in my hand. When I looked down, it was a number I didn't recognize.

"Hello," I said politely.

"Are you ready to give that bitch a divorce and come back where you belong?"

"Shanell, this game you're playing needs to stop! I will not be leaving my wife for you or any other woman. Get that shit out of your head! You fucked up when you put your hands on my daughter. You fucked up when you sent that bullshit to my house, and you messed up pretty bad when you destroyed my car. When I see you, I'm beating your ass!" I yelled into the phone.

"You promise?" She laughed as my doorbell rang. "You're not going to do shit to me, Wes."

I walked slowly to the door with the phone still up to my ear and snatched it open. Shanell stood on the porch with a black trench coat on with a matching red bra and panty set. The red high heels she had on her feet made her legs look longer than they were. The sight before me used to make my dick rise. Now I just wanted to choke the shit out of her and dump her fuckin' body in the woods.

"The fuck you doing at my house, Shanell?" I asked through clenched teeth. I tossed my phone on the table by the door and grilled her stupid ass.

"I wanted to see you, baby. Is that a problem?" she asked softly.

"Hell yeah, it's a problem! I live here with my wife, bitch! How the fuck did you find out where I live?" I was madder than a pit bull in a dogfight and I was restraining myself from reaching out to touch her dumb ass.

"You led me to your house," she said, smiling from ear to ear. "It was me and you before you had a muthafuckin' wife, Wes! Did you forget about that? Fuck that bitch. It was supposed to be me and you against the world. What happened to that shit, huh?"

Shanell was getting louder with every word that came out of her mouth. I didn't want any of the neighbors in my business, so I grabbed her by her neck and dragged her inside and closed the door. Dap walked out the kitchen and his eyebrows furrowed instantly.

"What the fuck you doing here, hoe?" he spewed at her.

"Hello to you too, Dap. Long time no see, bro. What brings you back to the Windy City?" Shanell smiled.

"Don't worry about me, bitch!"

"Brah, I got this," I said, holding up my hand. "Shanell, what do you want?"

"I want you to do what you promised, Wes. You said you would never leave me in the cold. It will forever be me and you. That's what the fuck I want." Shanell ran her hand up and down my chest and I slapped it down quickly.

"You're reneging on the agreement! I'm going to fuck with you and your family until you leave. You turned me into this person I've become! It's nobody's fault but yours, *Weston.* The more you try to push me away, the harder I'm going to come for what you love." She grinned.

"Faith is so beautiful, Wes. She's all I thought she would be." She smirked. "My baby belongs at home with her mommy and daddy, baby. Bring her back to me."

Shanell rubbed her hands up and down her breasts as she walked toward me. Placing her right hand in her panties, I could tell she was strumming her clit while staring into my eyes. The bitch was crazy as fuck and off her meds. The next sentence that fell from her lips made me snap.

"You know I could've killed her, right?" She chuckled.

I grabbed her by the throat and slammed her against the mirrored wall. Pulling my bitch from my pants, I pressed it against her nose while breathing heavily. "I will blow your fuckin' head off, bitch!" I said, slowly pushing my finger on the trigger.

"Brah, shoot that bitch now!" Dap said, walking toward us. "We can get rid of her body with no problem."

Shanell grabbed my hand and I thought she was trying to stop me from pulling the trigger. Her sick ass actually lowered the tip of the gun to her mouth and started sucking the nozzle like it was a dick. Her saliva dripped onto my hand and I hated the fact that my dick swelled in my shorts. Snapping back to reality, I revved back and smacked her across the temple with the butt of the gun.

"Get the fuck out, and don't ever show up to my house again. I have too much love for you to kill you, Shanell. If you ever come for my family again, I will blow your fuckin' head off. Now get the fuck out and go find somebody else to play with." Blood ran down the side of her head, but she smiled as she wiped at the blood with her sleeve.

"I'm going to leave, Wes. You have proven to me that there won't ever be anything between us again. I love you enough to let you be happy, even if it's not with me. Tell your wife, she has a good husband and she better cherish every day she has with you." Shanell stumbled out the door and got into her car. She sat in the driver's seat for a moment before pulling out of the driveway.

"Wes, are you stupid? You should've killed that bitch! I hope you didn't believe a damn thing she just said. Shanell gave you the opportunity to kill her and get away with it, and you let her psychotic ass walk! What the fuck is wrong with you?"

"Not now, Dap. I couldn't pull the trigger, okay? I couldn't do it," I said, closing and locking the door.

"I'm out of here. I don't know what the fuck you were thinking, but what you just did told me you have more feelings for Shanell than you let on. The bitch is going to come harder than before and once again, it will be on your conscience."

My brother left my home and I knew he was disappointed in me for sure. I had the chance to silence Shanell and fucked up by freezing.

I walked into the kitchen, cleaned up the remnants of the food I attempted to eat, and went upstairs.

Sitting in the middle of the bed, I sifted through the papers I had sprawled about on the bed and worked the remainder of the day. My mind kept shifting back to the incident with Shanell, and I knew I had made the biggest mistake of my life. As I worked through the rest of day, Justice had called to tell me she made it to Arizona. I didn't know how to tell her what happened with Shanell, so I didn't bring it up. Hopefully Dap didn't tell Tana, because it would definitely get back to my wife and she would be pissed all over again.

We spent time on Facetime and I had the chance to see my daughter and speak with Justice's parents before settling down for the night. My mind had to be free of all negative vibes for my meeting the next day. It was another big contract and I needed to ace it, for my sake. After finishing all the drawings needed along with my presentation, I took a shower and went to bed for the first time without my wife lying next to me.

***

When I stepped out of the steamy bathroom, I went to the closet and selected a navy-blue Versace suit, a light blue dress shirt, with a matching navy-blue tie with light blue stripes. Removing the towel from my waist, I pulled my boxer briefs over my hips and sat on the edge of the bed to put on my socks.

My phone chimed and I continued to get dressed. As I slipped my feet into my black Stacy Adams shoes, my phone chimed back to back and I knew right away it was Shanell's ass on bullshit early in the morning. The image of her deep throating the nozzle of my gun was on the forefront of my mind. I walked to my side of the bed and picked up my phone.

(773)555-1977: Good morning dummy. I knew for sure I was a goner yesterday but you further let me know that you still love me.

(773)555-1977: Bring Faith home to me, Wes. You know I would never hurt her.

(773)555-1977: I love you to death, Mr. King. And I mean that in a literal sense LOL

(773)555-1977: You should've killed me. Let the games begin, muthafucker!

I pressed on the icon to call the number back and I should've known, it was another burner phone. Shanell had never acted out in this manner before and it was a for sure sign that she needed help badly. Gathering my briefcase, I scooped up my keys and made my way down the stairs and out the door to my car.

The first thing I did after getting settled in the driver's seat was connect my phone to the Bluetooth. It was pretty early and I didn't know if my sister was wake, but she was about to be in a few seconds. I hit her name in my contacts and listened to the phone ring.

"Why are you calling me so early, Wes?" she asked groggily.

"Call your fuckin' friend before she comes up missing! I spared her fuckin' life yesterday and she still wants to fuck with me."

"Like I told Dad last night, I'm in Michigan and have nothing to do with what's going on in Chicago. I will talk to Shanell when I get there tomorrow. Do not, and I repeat, do not call me again about your problems," she said, hanging up on me.

I drove the rest of the way to work in silence because Bria was being too calm about this situation with Shanell and I didn't like it. I helped her on many occasions and this was the thanks I got from her. Maybe Dap was right, she had no loyalty when it came to her family and I didn't know why. I was going to ask when she touched down for sure.

As I pulled into the garage, I parked and hurried to the elevator. I stepped off and walked past Charlotte, mumbling a dry "good morning". My mood was somber and I didn't want to be in the office. I should've been in Arizona with my wife. I sat behind my desk and logged into my computer to check my emails. Reading over the email from my boss, Mr. Williamson, I noticed the meeting had been moved up to noon.

There was a knock on the door and I knew it was Stewart.

"Come on in, Stew," I said without looking up.

The door and closed without the usual greeting Stew gave when he entered my office. When I looked up from my computer, Shanell stood in front of my desk with a sinister look on her face. I shook my head. I couldn't believe the balls this bitch had. Somebody gave her a cup of courage because she was getting bolder by the day.

"Shanell, what are you doing here?" I asked, standing to my feet.

"Sit yo' ass down, Wes. I'm tired of you playing with my emotions," she sneered.

"I'm not doing shit!" I yelled. "This is my place of work and you come here with this bullshit."

Walking around my desk, Shanell pulled her hand out of her pocket and produced a handgun, stopping me in my tracks.

"That's what I thought. Sit the fuck down, because you're going to hear me out without putting your hands on me. You're not the only one that has a gun, nigga." I eased back to the chair behind my desk and sat down slowly. "I want us to be together again. This will be the last time I plead with you to take me back. I'm all out of apologies, Wes."

"You're fuckin' crazy, bitch!" I sneered.

"Nah, you haven't seen crazy. Meet me at the Omni hotel at six o'clock or you will regret the day you met me."

"It's too late for that." I laughed. "I regretted the day I rescued yo' ass when you touched my daughter."

"She's our daughter! Faith is the daughter we planned together and I want her home, Wes. Meet me at the hotel like I told you. Six o'clock, don't be late," she said, putting the gun in her pocket as opened the door to leave. "Don't play with me. My patience has run out fuckin' with you, Wes."

Picking up the receiver to the desk phone, I dialed the number to security and the line was busy. I pressed the button and tried again a few minutes later then Earl answered. "Citywide Security."

"Earl, it's Weston. Do you see a woman in a black North face coat with tight jeans on in the lobby?"

"Man, baby girl was right! I tried to holla—"

"Earl, is she still in the building?" I yelled.

"Damn, man, nawl, shorty just left out the automatic doors. Why, you need me to catch her?" he asked.

"No, I need you to tell me what name she signed under." I heard him rustling through papers until he came back on the line.

"Okay, she signed in as um, S. King. Damn, is that your sister or something, boss? I need to get next to shawty."

Earl was getting on my nerves with his thirsty ass. He was thinking about smashing and I was trying to talk about a serious matter.

"That's not my sister and her last name is not King! She is a crazy bitch that is no longer allowed in this building. Keep your eyes off her ass and on her face. If you see her again, escort her out and call the police. Is that understood?"

"Damn, what happened?"

"It doesn't matter, fuck! Just do what I ask and make note of the shit," I said, hanging up on his stupid ass.

I made calls to the auto shop and the insurance company to check on the status of my car. There was no use trying to repair it, so it was totaled out. I went back to checking my emails until my meeting started. Stewart had to come get me from my office minutes before the meeting started because I lost track of time.

Three hours later, another big company was using the services of Citywide to conduct their business. I was sitting on top of the world in the architecture industry and I was loving it. Stewart ordered food and refreshments to celebrate until it was punch out time. Justice called and I told her the great news because when I won a client over, there was always a bonus in store for me.

"Congratulations, babe! I won't hold you. Enjoy your victory and I'll talk to you later. Love you."

"Thank you and I love you back," I said, smiling from ear to ear.

Stewart walked over, hitting me on the shoulder. "Let's blow this joint and really celebrate. We can go down the street to the bar for Happy Hour because this sparkling cider is not going to do it. I need something stronger."

"I agree. Let me hit my brother so he can join us, then we can leave," I said, pulling out my phone.

Me: Aye, bro, I won another client over and it's a reason to celebrate. Meet me at Mary's down the street from my job. Drinks are on me.

As I waited for Dap to respond, I went into my office and gathered all of my belongings. I met Stewart at the elevators, then we rode down to the garage together. Parting ways, I jumped in my ride and pulled out of the garage slowly so Stewart could catch up. Once he was behind me, I drove off and made a right turn down the street.

Chapter 19
Shanell

Something in my gut told me Wes was not going to show up to the hotel. I had a trick for his ass because I didn't know when he was going to leave work, so instead of leaving, I parked my car in the very garage of his job. Wes had never taken his parking pass out of my car from a while back. It came in handy that day.

I laid back in my car all day, waiting patiently for Wes to leave for the day while playing games and watching shows on my phone. I dozed off a couple times, but never for too long. When Wes and his colleague Stewart stepped off the elevator, I waited until one of them started his car before I cranked mine up too. Wes pulled out first, waiting for Stewart then he pulled out and that was my chance to get behind Stewart.

I followed them about three blocks until I saw both of them pull into valet at Mary's. It would've been stupid for me to go into valet so instead, I went around the corner and parked in one of the cheap parking lots, where I paid ten dollars for three hours. I knew what I had planned wouldn't take three hours. I just hoped my plan worked.

I walked back and ducked into Mary's, and it was pretty crowded for an early Friday evening. I blended in with the many folks that crowded around the bar and made my way to a dark corner. I could see everything going on in the establishment and spotted Wes and Stewart sitting on the other side by the window. The barmaid had just given them three shots and a couple Coronas apiece.

I kept my eyes on the woman. I sat and watched as she worked the room with a smile on her face. Twenty minutes into their celebration, I saw Wes getting ready to down his last shot. It was time for me to make my move. The barmaid was walking quickly past me and I reached out to stop her.

"Excuse me. The guys by the window are low on their drinks. I would like to send them another round of double shots on me. Can you help me?" I asked sweetly.

"Sure. You don't see too many women buying guys drinks. You must have your eye on the dark-skinned black guy, huh?"

"Yeah, he is fine, hunni." I laughed.

"Well, you may have a better shot at him than me. He turned me down quick as hell. I guess because he doesn't like cream in his coffee," she said snidely.

"I know a way you can get back at him for rejecting you," I smirked. "Put one of these in his drink," I said, holding out a Xanax pill.

"I'm not losing my job for you, lady," she shot back. "I'm going to inform my boss about what you asked me to do." She turned to walk away and I grabbed her by the arm and stood from my seat as I dug deep into my purse.

"Susan," I said, reading her name tag as I pushed the nozzle of my gun into her stomach. "I will blow your mutha-fuckin' large intestines through your back and make sure the only way you'll ever be able to shit is in a bag. I'm willing to give you five hundred dollars to deliver the drink to the man you have been lusting over, or I can end your life before the end of the night. Your choice."

The terror on her face gave my clit a heartbeat. My nipples hardened and I was ready to fuck. "What do you say? Are you in?" Susan shook her head vigorously up and down. I pushed the gun deeper in her stomach as I leaned in, licking her earlobe. "Remember what I said. Don't say shit to anybody, or die."

I stepped back and watched Susan pour the drinks as I twirled the pill between my fingers. She came back to where I stood and I dropped the pill in one of the glasses, swirling it around in the glass. Once it was dissolved, I put the money for the drinks on the tray and held up five crisp one hundred-dollar bills. I tucked the money down the front of her shirt and blew her a kiss. Nodding her head, she delivered the drinks and stood talking to Wes.

Taking that opportunity to duck into the bathroom, I washed my hands and checked my makeup before leaving out. Susan was standing by the table and I crept behind her, palming her ass. "Did he drink it?" I asked, squeezing her cheek firmly.

"Yes, yes, his friend left while you were in the bathroom but the other guy looks like he is going to have a problem getting home."

"No, I got him covered. Thank you for your help," I said, walking over to the table where Wes was sitting. Susan was fine and sexy, but she better not play with me because I had no problem killing her pale ass.

Wes's head was bobbing as he tried to hold it upright. I slid in the chair and smiled at him as saliva dripped from his lip. Reaching over, I wiped his mouth with my finger and he looked up the best he could. Wes squinted his eyes and blinked uncontrollably as he fought to focus on my face.

"Shanell?" he slurred. "What's wrong with me?"

"You had too much to drink, babe. We agreed to meet here and you are fucked up. How long have you been drinking?" I asked to see how he would respond.

"I don't know. I didn't have much to drink. You know I love you, right? I've missed you, Nell."

I'd been waiting a long time to hear those words fall from his mouth. I loved Wes too, and it was a shame I had to drug

187

him to hear him admit what I already knew. Trying hard not to laugh, I watched him for a few minutes before I set the second part of my plan in motion.

"Where are your keys? I have to get you home because you are in no condition to drive."

"They're with valet, but the ticket is in my suit jacket. But I can't get it," he slurred. "If I move my hand. My head is going to fall off."

"I got you, baby," I said, standing to get the valet ticket. I'll be right back," I said, making my way out of the bar. Handing the ticket to the attendant, I told him I'd be right back. As I walked back into the bar, I ran into Susan. "Hey, I need a man to help me get him in his car. Is one available?"

The bitch stared at me like she was about to say something smart until I patted my bag. Reaching inside, I stepped closer to her so I could whisper in her ear. "Give me your fuckin' license. I don't trust you to keep your mouth closed."

Susan eyes shifted and I pulled my bitch out and her eyes almost popped out of her head. She put her hand in her apron and brought out a wallet that held the five hundred dollars I'd given here inside. She showed me her license and I used my phone to take a picture of it before handing it back.

"If I hear anything about what I've done tonight, I will be paying you a visit. Now get someone to help me put his ass in the car!" I snarled.

I walked back to the table to retrieve Wes, and one of the bartenders came over to give me some help. It took no time to get Wes situated in the passenger seat of his car. I buckled him in the seatbelt and ran around and hopped inside. My pussy was doing the salsa with anticipation of what was to come. Rush hour was a thing of the past and it was light traffic on the expressway. We made it to the suburbs in twenty minutes flat.

After pushing the garage opener that was attached to the sun visor, I pulled his car inside. Wes was nodding like a crackhead, but I could tell he was eager to sleep. That wasn't going to happen because he had what I'd been craving for the past couple months. I opened the door and unsnapped his seatbelt, then helped Wes maneuver his way out of the car. He was walking slowly as he held on to my waist and I followed his lead.

Once inside, the alarm beeped and I panicked. "What's the code to the alarm, baby?" I asked frantically.

"5170," he slurred.

Forgetting he was unstable, I let him go and made a dash for the front door. I entered the code with two seconds remaining before it would've gone off, I heard a loud bang in the kitchen. I ran into the room and Wes was struggling to stay on his feet as he held onto the open freezer door of the refrigerator.

Wes used my body to rest against and we started walking through the house. He turned left and went down a short hall to a door that was closed. When I turned the knob, there was a queen-sized bed in the room and that was all I needed. Sitting Wes on the bed, I helped him remove his clothes and shoes. Falling back on the bed, his head slumped to the side and his eyes closed.

I didn't care if he wasn't coherent. I was about to get the dick that I missed. Putting my purse and phone on the dresser, I walked back to the bed and pulled down his briefs. Wes's pipe sprang out like a jack in the box and my mouth started salivating. Getting on my knees, I buried my head between his legs and sucked his dick like never before.

His moans got louder with every suction of my jaw and he found some way to palm the back of my head for me to go deeper. "Oh, shit! Yeah, just like that." Wes lifted his hips off the bed and fed me roughly as he pulled my hair at scalp.

"Aaaaahhhhh, fuck!" he groaned as he shot his semen down my throat and released me.

My kitty was soaking the seat of my thong and I was ready for him to fill me up. The pill I gave him had his member sitting at attention even though he had already nutted hard. Hurrying to get out of my clothes, I mounted his rod and exhaled. Rocking my hips back and forth, I caught a rhythm and rode with it. The way the tip of his dick hit my G-spot, I could feel an orgasm forcing its way out.

"Oh, yeah. Fuck me, baby! Fuck me!"

Wes gripped my hips as I laid flat on his chest and kissed him with all the love in my body. He returned the kiss and pulled my hips forward on his stick. Using his right thumb, he strummed my clit and I started bouncing slowing up and down. My stomach muscles tightened and I squirted all over him and the bed.

"Aaaah, shit! Oooooowweee!"

I kept riding him slowly because he was still hard as a rock and I wanted it all. Wes was going to cum in me as many times as I wanted because there was no way he could stop me. I bit his lower lip, then turned around in the reverse cowgirl position, grabbing my ankles. Wes grabbed my ass cheeks and slipped a finger in my ass and I lost it.

"You know I love that shit, baby! Go deeper, Wes," I said, reaching back, forcing his finger further up my ass. "Yes! Yes! Yes!" I screamed.

"You being real freaky tonight, Justice. I love that shit."

Hearing him say his bitch-ass wife's name pissed me off, but I had to get another nut.

"Whose dick is this?" I moaned.

"It's yours, Justice, baby. It's yours."

Grinding faster on his dick, I moaned loudly and asked the question again. "Whose dick is this, Wes?" I asked, looking back at him.

"Justice, it's yours, baby!" he screamed. "I'm about to cum, Justice! Oh shit, baby, I'm cummin'!"

The way he dug his nails into my waist, he was holding on for dear life and I was riding him like he was a stallion. When he let go of his load, I was ready to leave because hearing him call out another woman's name hurt my heart.

Getting up out of the bed, I dressed fast and before I grabbed my phone and purse, I wrote him a note and left.

Meesha

Chapter 20
Dap

I didn't want shit to do with my brother after the cowardly shit he pulled with that bitch Shanell. Wes had her ass right in front of him and did not shoot her muthafuckin' ass. When he texted me to come celebrate with him at the bar, I didn't even respond because I didn't care. But when Tana called me Saturday afternoon saying Wes wasn't answering his phone, I went straight to the house to check on him. His car wasn't in the driveway and that bothered me.

Using the key Justice gave me, I entered the house and went straight upstairs. When I got to Wes and Justice's bedroom, the bed was made and nothing was out of place. I checked the bathroom, and it, too, was empty. At that point I was panicking because no one had heard from my brother since the night before.

I ran out of the bedroom and went to the nursery and it, too, was empty. I kept moving and went back downstairs and checked the garage. Wes's car was parked perfectly inside, but he wasn't anywhere in the house. Thinking about the night I stayed the night, I remembered Tana slept in the room downstairs by the laundry room. Jogging in that direction, I pushed the door open and saw Wes lying horizontally across the bed with his dick out.

Because he was snoring loudly, I knew he was alright. I threw the blanket over him and the scent of sex filled my nostrils. I turned to walk back out of the room when a piece of paper caught my eye. Snatching it up, I left to let him continue to sleep off whatever he did to get him that fucked up. Before I made it back to the living room, my phone was ringing and it was Tana.

"Hey, Tana."

"Did you find Wes?"

"Yes, he's still sleeping. Tell Justice he's okay. I'm at the house and I'm going to stay here until he wakes up." I said, unfolding the paper. Reading the message before me, I tuned Tana out as my heart started beating fast.

Wes, I had a good time tonight and I missed you just as much as you missed me. Find out who bought the drink before you drink it next time. LOL. You still fuck me better than anyone and I love you too. Just so you know, we didn't use protection but it was worth every stroke. Until next time, baby.

Shanell

"What the fuck did you do, Wes?" I screamed to myself.

"Donovan!" Tana said loudly.

"Yeah, I'm here. I gotta go to the bathroom, I'll call you back."

"Okay. Are you sure everything is alright?" She asked.

"I won't know until my brother wakes up. I've never seen him drunk like this. But let me drain the willie and I'll hit you back."

After hanging up the phone, I went to the kitchen and scooped some ice into bowl and filled it with water. Marching to the guest room, I snatched the blanket back and dumped the bowl of ice water all over my brother.

"Cold! That shit is cold!" He screamed.

"Wes, get the fuck up!"

He looked at me angrily and sat straight up. "Oh my God, my head is pounding," he groaned, holding his fingers to his temple.

"I need to know what happened to you, brah. What did you do last night?"

"The last thing I remember was having drinks with Stewart at the bar. We were celebrating my accomplishments in winning a new client. Both of us had a couple drinks and the barmaid came over with a drink some woman bought for us. After drinking the last drink, Stewart left and I don't remember shit after that."

"Brah, Shanell was the woman that bought the drink and she slipped something in it."

"How do you know that? Did you help her?" he asked

"Why the fuck would I help her drug you? The bitch was in this house and the two of you had a good old time having sex. Unprotected at that."

Wes looked down at his body for the first time since he woke up. There was dried up cum on several parts of his body and the stains were evident on the blanket. His clothes were sprawled across the floor and there was a black thong in the corner by the door.

"I didn't knowingly sleep with her, Dap. Justice can't find out about this shit. She will leave me for sure."

Handing him the note, he read it and dropped to his knees. "I'm going to kill that bitch, brah," he cried.

"I told you to kill her when you had the chance. You were the one that gave her a second chance to fuck your life up. She's not going to stop until she destroys you, Wes. We have to find her and put an end to this bullshit." I paced back and forth in front of the bed.

"Tomorrow Beverly is throwing you and Justice a baby shower. I wasn't supposed to tell you because they wanted it to be a surprise. I'm telling you because as you know, Bria is coming in for the party. That would be your chance to corner her to get answers about Shanell's whereabouts."

Wes wrapped the blanket around his waist and walked toward the door. "What time is this baby shower?" he asked.

"It's starts at two. I'm supposed to pick Justice up and bring y'all to the venue. Tana already knows about it, but she decided to go with Justice. That's the reason Bria flew in, so she could help with the setup."

"Okay, bet, wake me at noon. Get me lots of water because I need to flush whatever Shanell put in my drink out of my system. I need to go back to sleep."

Wes headed toward the stairs and I went to the kitchen. "Bro, make sure to wash your ass before you get in that bed. I'm going to wash the sheets in the guest room to destroy all of the evidence. Your secret is safe with me."

"I love you, Dap. Thanks."

"Yo' ass been telling the wrong muthafuckas you love them. Be careful with that shit," I laughed.

"Fuck you and bring me water."

***

Wes slept like a baby and I took the opportunity to go home to pack a bag. When I returned, I made the bed in the guest room, but I got comfortable on the couch. I set my alarm for eleven o'clock because I had to pick the ladies up from the airport. I turned the TV on. As I watched the highlights of the basketball games on SportsCenter, I drifted off to sleep myself.

The smell of sausage woke me from my slumber and I looked over the back of the couch into the kitchen. Wes was dressed as he stood over the stove cooking. I swung my feet onto the floor and stood up, cracking every bone in my body. Snatching my bag from the floor by the door, I went into the bathroom to take care of my hygiene.

Wes was sitting down eating as I entered the kitchen. I grabbed a piece of toast and the rest of the eggs onto a plate and sat down across from my brother. "How are you feeling?" I asked, taking a bite out of the bread.

196

"Better than yesterday. I can't believe Shanell got over on me."

"Psst, I can. The bitch is doing whatever she can to fuck with you. Stop under estimating her crazy ass, bro. Shanell is a dangerous species and she's out for blood. You don't even know what she gave you, and that's not good at all."

"I know that now. I'm done feeling sorry for her. What time is my wife landing?" he asked. I looked at the clock on the wall and cursed under my breath.

"Their plan lands at twelve-thirty! We have forty-five minutes to make it to Midway. And that's only if we leave now! In other words, let's go!" I said, jumping up with my plate in hand.

Rising the plate, I threw it in the dishwasher, grabbed my bag, and left out the door. Sitting in my car, I waited for Wes to exit. The garage door raised up and I reversed my ride so he could get out. Switching gears, I put my ride in drive and headed toward the expressway.

We made it to the airport in just enough time to see Justice and Tana walking outside. I jumped out and grabbed Tana's and Justice's bags and Wes helped with Faith. I helped Justice into the car and told Wes to follow me as I led Tana to my whip.

"How was the flight?" I asked, pulling off.

"It was okay. A lot of turbulence, but nothing too bad. What about you?" she asked, looking at me with a smile.

"You know me, I'm always good. Are you ready for the shower?"

"Yes! Beverly has been driving me crazy the entire time I've been gone, but the end result is beautiful. I can't wait for Justice to see it. I got confirmation from former classmates, her coworkers, and some of her family that they were going to be there. Did y'all find Shanell?"

"No. before the day is over, we will know where to start looking though."

"I hope so, because Justice is ready to go back to work and I don't want to have to worry about Shanell going after her. She's crazy, Donovan."

"Tell me something I don't know already," I said, pushing the gas.

It took damn near forty minutes to get to the venue and the parking lot was packed. Justice was about to be surprised when she got inside. I found a park and Wes found one three cars over. Tana and I got out and waited for Wes to get Faith out of the backseat. I shot Beverly a text letting her know we were on our way inside.

"Where are we?" Justice asked curiously.

"One of my friends is having an anniversary party and I told him I would come through for a minute. We won't be in long," I replied.

"Wes, I'm tired. We will be here thirty minutes tops and then we have to go. I need to take a shower and get a nap in."

"Okay, baby. Thirty minutes," he said, kissing the side of her head.

When we entered the building, the music was bumping and it sound like everyone was having a good time. When I opened the door to the main room, the music stopped and I let Wes and Justice enter first. A projector on the wall started playing a video with pictures of Wes and Justice on their wedding day.

"Surprise!" everybody in attendance yelled.

Justice looked back at me and punched me in the chest. "You knew about this all along." She laughed as she hugged me. Beverly and Pops walked over and hugged all of us before taking Faith to show her off.

The room was decorated in pink and white everything. There were huge pictures of Faith and her parents hanging on the walls. The music started back up, but it wasn't as loud as before. We were all mingling when the sound in the room changed from Chris Brown's "Heat" to sexual moans.

The projector that were displaying images of Justice and Wes, turned into a full fledge Pornhub video. Shanell was sucking Wes off before she climbed on his joint, making her ass clap. The color drained from Wes's face and Justice had tears running down her face.

"You ain't shit! I'm done with this shit, muthafucka!" Justice said, turning around to walk out of the venue. "And you knew all about this shit but smiled in my face like it was nothing. Fuck both of y'all!" she said yelling at me before, running out of the room.

To Be Continued...
Paid in Karma 2
Coming Soon

Submission Guideline

Submit the first three chapters of your completed manuscript to ldpsubmissions@gmail.com, subject line: Your book's title. The manuscript must be in a .doc file and sent as an attachment. Document should be in Times New Roman, double spaced and in size 12 font. Also, provide your synopsis and full contact information. If sending multiple submissions, they must each be in a separate email.

Have a story but no way to send it electronically? You can still submit to LDP/Ca$h Presents. Send in the first three chapters, written or typed, of your completed manuscript to:

LDP: Submissions Dept
Po Box 870494
Mesquite, Tx 75187

DO NOT send original manuscript. Must be a duplicate.

Provide your synopsis and a cover letter containing your full contact information.

Thanks for considering LDP and Ca$h Presents.

Coming Soon from Lock Down Publications/Ca$h Presents

BOW DOWN TO MY GANGSTA

By **Ca$h**

TORN BETWEEN TWO

By **Coffee**

THE STREETS STAINED MY SOUL **II**

By **Marcellus Allen**

BLOOD OF A BOSS **VI**

SHADOWS OF THE GAME II

By **Askari**

LOYAL TO THE GAME **IV**

By **T.J. & Jelissa**

A DOPEBOY'S PRAYER **II**

By **Eddie "Wolf" Lee**

IF LOVING YOU IS WRONG… **III**

By **Jelissa**

TRUE SAVAGE **VII**

MIDNIGHT CARTEL

DOPE BOY MAGIC II

By **Chris Green**

BLAST FOR ME **III**

DUFFLE BAG CARTEL **IV**

HEARTLESS GOON **IV**

A SAVAGE DOPEBOY II

DRUG LORDS III

By **Ghost**

Meesha

A HUSTLER'S DECEIT III

KILL ZONE **II**

BAE BELONGS TO ME III

SOUL OF A MONSTER III

By **Aryanna**

THE COST OF LOYALTY **III**

By **Kweli**

THE SAVAGE LIFE III

CHAINED TO THE STREETS II

By **J-Blunt**

KING OF NEW YORK V

COKE KINGS IV

BORN HEARTLESS IV

By **T.J. Edwards**

GORILLAZ IN THE BAY V

De'Kari

THE STREETS ARE CALLING II

Duquie Wilson

KINGPIN KILLAZ IV

STREET KINGS III

PAID IN BLOOD III

CARTEL KILLAZ IV

Hood Rich

SINS OF A HUSTLA II

ASAD

TRIGGADALE III

Elijah R. Freeman

202

KINGZ OF THE GAME V

Playa Ray

SLAUGHTER GANG IV

RUTHLESS HEART II

By Willie Slaughter

THE HEART OF A SAVAGE II

By Jibril Williams

FUK SHYT II

By Blakk Diamond

THE DOPEMAN'S BODYGAURD II

By Tranay Adams

TRAP GOD II

By Troublesome

YAYO III

A SHOOTER'S AMBITION II

By S. Allen

GHOST MOB

Stilloan Robinson

KINGPIN DREAMS II

By Paper Boi Rari

CREAM

By Yolanda Moore

SON OF A DOPE FIEND II

By Renta

FOREVER GANGSTA II

By Adrian Dulan

LOYALTY AIN'T PROMISED

By Keith Williams

THE PRICE YOU PAY FOR LOVE II

By Destiny Skai

THE LIFE OF A HOOD STAR

By Rashia Wilson

TOE TAGZ II

By Ah'Million

CONFESSIONS OF A GANGSTA II

By Nicholas Lock

PAID IN KARMA II

By **Meesha**

Available Now

RESTRAINING ORDER **I & II**

By **CA$H & Coffee**

LOVE KNOWS NO BOUNDARIES **I II & III**

By **Coffee**

RAISED AS A GOON I, II, III & IV

BRED BY THE SLUMS I, II, III

BLAST FOR ME I & II

ROTTEN TO THE CORE I II III

A BRONX TALE I, II, III

DUFFEL BAG CARTEL I II III

HEARTLESS GOON

A SAVAGE DOPEBOY

HEARTLESS GOON I II III

DRUG LORDS I II

By **Ghost**

LAY IT DOWN **I & II**

LAST OF A DYING BREED

BLOOD STAINS OF A SHOTTA I & II III

By **Jamaica**

LOYAL TO THE GAME

LOYAL TO THE GAME II

LOYAL TO THE GAME III

LIFE OF SIN I, II III

By **TJ & Jelissa**

BLOODY COMMAS I & II

SKI MASK CARTEL I II & III

KING OF NEW YORK I II,III IV

RISE TO POWER I II III

COKE KINGS I II III

BORN HEARTLESS I II III

By **T.J. Edwards**

IF LOVING HIM IS WRONG…I & II

LOVE ME EVEN WHEN IT HURTS I II III

By **Jelissa**

WHEN THE STREETS CLAP BACK I & II III

By **Jibril Williams**

A DISTINGUISHED THUG STOLE MY HEART I II & III

LOVE SHOULDN'T HURT I II III IV

RENEGADE BOYS I II III IV

PAID IN KARMA

By **Meesha**

A GANGSTER'S CODE I &, II III

A GANGSTER'S SYN I II III

THE SAVAGE LIFE I II

CHAINED TO THE STREETS

By **J-Blunt**

PUSH IT TO THE LIMIT

By **Bre' Hayes**

BLOOD OF A BOSS **I, II, III, IV, V**

SHADOWS OF THE GAME

By **Askari**

THE STREETS BLEED MURDER **I, II & III**

THE HEART OF A GANGSTA I II& III

By **Jerry Jackson**

CUM FOR ME

CUM FOR ME 2

CUM FOR ME 3

CUM FOR ME 4

CUM FOR ME 5

An **LDP Erotica Collaboration**

BRIDE OF A HUSTLA **I II & II**

THE FETTI GIRLS **I, II& III**

CORRUPTED BY A GANGSTA I, II III, IV

BLINDED BY HIS LOVE

THE PRICE YOU PAY FOR LOVE

By **Destiny Skai**

WHEN A GOOD GIRL GOES BAD

Paid in Karma

By **Adrienne**
THE COST OF LOYALTY I II
By Kweli
A GANGSTER'S REVENGE **I II III & IV**
THE BOSS MAN'S DAUGHTERS
THE BOSS MAN'S DAUGHTERS II
THE BOSSMAN'S DAUGHTERS III
THE BOSSMAN'S DAUGHTERS IV
THE BOSS MAN'S DAUGHTERS **V**
A SAVAGE LOVE **I & II**
BAE BELONGS TO ME I II
A HUSTLER'S DECEIT I, II, III
WHAT BAD BITCHES DO I, II, III
SOUL OF A MONSTER I II
KILL ZONE
By **Aryanna**
A KINGPIN'S AMBITON
A KINGPIN'S AMBITION **II**
I MURDER FOR THE DOUGH
By **Ambitious**
TRUE SAVAGE
TRUE SAVAGE II
TRUE SAVAGE **III**
TRUE SAVAGE **IV**
TRUE SAVAGE **V**
TRUE SAVAGE **VI**
DOPE BOY MAGIC

MIDNIGHT CARTEL
By **Chris Green**
A DOPEBOY'S PRAYER
By **Eddie "Wolf" Lee**
THE KING CARTEL **I, II & III**
By **Frank Gresham**
THESE NIGGAS AIN'T LOYAL **I, II & III**
By **Nikki Tee**
GANGSTA SHYT **I II &III**
By **CATO**
THE ULTIMATE BETRAYAL
By **Phoenix**
BOSS'N UP **I , II & III**
By **Royal Nicole**
I LOVE YOU TO DEATH
By Destiny J
I RIDE FOR MY HITTA
I STILL RIDE FOR MY HITTA
By **Misty Holt**
LOVE & CHASIN' PAPER
By **Qay Crockett**
TO DIE IN VAIN
SINS OF A HUSTLA
By **ASAD**
BROOKLYN HUSTLAZ
By **Boogsy Morina**
BROOKLYN ON LOCK I & II

Paid in Karma

By **Sonovia**

GANGSTA CITY

By **Teddy Duke**

A DRUG KING AND HIS DIAMOND I & II III

A DOPEMAN'S RICHES

HER MAN, MINE'S TOO I, II

CASH MONEY HO'S

By Nicole Goosby

TRAPHOUSE KING **I II & III**

KINGPIN KILLAZ I II III

STREET KINGS I II

PAID IN BLOOD **I II**

CARTEL KILLAZ I II III

By **Hood Rich**

LIPSTICK KILLAH **I, II, III**

CRIME OF PASSION I II & III

By **Mimi**

STEADY MOBBN' **I, II, III**

THE STREETS STAINED MY SOUL

By **Marcellus Allen**

WHO SHOT YA **I, II, III**

SON OF A DOPE FIEND

Renta

GORILLAZ IN THE BAY **I II III IV**

DE'KARI

TRIGGADALE I II

Elijah R. Freeman

Meesha

GOD BLESS THE TRAPPERS I, II, III
THESE SCANDALOUS STREETS I, II, III
FEAR MY GANGSTA I, II, III
THESE STREETS DON'T LOVE NOBODY I, II
BURY ME A G I, II, III, IV, V
A GANGSTA'S EMPIRE I, II, III, IV
THE DOPEMAN'S BODYGAURD

Tranay Adams
THE STREETS ARE CALLING

Duquie Wilson
MARRIED TO A BOSS... I II III

By Destiny Skai & Chris Green
KINGZ OF THE GAME I II III IV

Playa Ray
SLAUGHTER GANG I II III
RUTHLESS HEART

By Willie Slaughter
THE HEART OF A SAVAGE

By Jibril Williams
FUK SHYT

By Blakk Diamond
DON'T F#CK WITH MY HEART I II

By Linnea
ADDICTED TO THE DRAMA I II III

By Jamila
YAYO I II
A SHOOTER'S AMBITION

By S. Allen
TRAP GOD
By Troublesome
FOREVER GANGSTA
By Adrian Dulan
TOE TAGZ
By Ah'Million
KINGPIN DREAMS
By Paper Boi Rari
CONFESSIONS OF A GANGSTA
By Nicholas Lock

Meesha

BOOKS BY LDP'S CEO, CA$H

TRUST IN NO MAN

TRUST IN NO MAN 2

TRUST IN NO MAN 3

BONDED BY BLOOD

SHORTY GOT A THUG

THUGS CRY

THUGS CRY 2

THUGS CRY 3

TRUST NO BITCH

TRUST NO BITCH 2

TRUST NO BITCH 3

TIL MY CASKET DROPS

RESTRAINING ORDER

RESTRAINING ORDER 2

IN LOVE WITH A CONVICT

Coming Soon

BONDED BY BLOOD 2

BOW DOWN TO MY GANGSTA

Paid in Karma